Fatal Attraction

A Thriller in Two Acts

by Bernard Slade

A SAMUEL FRENCH ACTING EDITION

SAMUEL FRENCH

FOUNDED 1830

New York Hollywood London Toronto

SAMUELFRENCH.COM

FATAL ATTRACTION was first produced in London by Duncan C. Weldon with Paul Gregg and Lionel Becker in association with Jerome Minskoff and Joseph P. Harris at the Theatre Royal Haymarket on the 26th of November, 1985. The production was directed by David Gilmore and designed by Roger Glossop with lighting by Bill Bray. The cast was as follows:

BLAIR GRIFFIN	Susannah York
MORGAN RICHARDS	David Baron
TONY LOMBARDI	Nick Brimble
SERGEANT DORIS AYLESWORTH	Jocelyn Cunningham
LIEUTENANT GUS BRADEN	Denis Quilley
MAGGIE STRATTON	Kate Harper

FATAL ATTRACTION was given its North American premiere at the St. Lawrence Centre Theatre in Toronto, Canada on November 8th, 1984. The production was directed by Tom Troupe with scenery and lighting by Gerry Hariton and Vicki Baral. The cast was as follows:

BLAIR GRIFFIN	Dawn Wells
MORGAN RICHARDS	Robin Ward
TONY LOMBARDI	Tony Noll
SERGEANT DORIS AYLESWORTH	Jayne Eastwood
LIEUTENANT GUS BRADEN	Ken Howard
MAGGIE STRATTON	Bette Ford

PRODUCTION NOTE

The jacuzzi can be constructed in a number of ways. If the stage is equipped with a trap, the ideal solution is to sink a plastic shell into the stage and use an electronically operated sliding wooden top.

If it is not possible to cut a hole in the stage, a simple method is to design the floor of the set on two different levels with the upstage part of the floor about two feet higher than the downstage level. The jacuzzi opening can be situated in this higher level or platform which will create enough crawl space underneath to conceal a body. A sliding top can be operated either mechanically by a winch or manually by a stagehand from under the jacuzzi top.

Dry ice can be used to disguise the fact that there is no water in the jacuzzi.

SETTING

The entire action of the play takes place over a period of three days in late October in the living room of a remote Nantucket beach house.

CAST
(*in order of appearance*)

BLAIR GRIFFIN — A fragile looking child-woman in her mid-thirties.

MORGAN RICHARDS — Blair's husband. Mid-forties. Attractive.

TONY LOMBARDI — An intense, kinetic thirty-five.

SERGEANT DORIS AYLESWORTH — Thirties. Pleasant-looking, bright, nice sense of humor.

LIEUTENANT GUS BRADEN — A flawed, idiosyncratic wreck of a man in his early fifties.

MAGGIE STRATTEN — 35-45. Very beautiful, warm, likeable.

Fatal Attraction

ACT ONE

SCENE 1

.THE TIME: *Mid afternoon of a cloudy late October day in the present.*

THE PLACE: *The living room of a compact remote beach house on the bluffs overlooking the ocean on the island of Nantucket. The front door to the house is Downstage Left, there is an entrance to a partially visible kitchen in the Upstage wall and a flight of stairs ascending to a landing that runs across the back wall and leads to a nonvisible bedroom and studio. The room has wooden pegged and grooved floors decorated with throw rugs, there is an often used fireplace on one wall and a curtained window on the other. Some wooden beams containing some potted plants span the room below the vaulted sky-lighted roof. The room is furnished with comfortable, English country antiques and includes a chintz sofa, chairs, a table used for eating, and a stereo. The over-flowing bookshelves and the other books and classical record albums casually piled around the room help give the place the look of an unstudied, personalized, hideaway of someone with cultivated tastes. There are some children's dolls scattered around the room.*

AT RISE: *The room is empty. The stereo is playing a recording of "Gymnopedies II" by Satie. After a moment, BLAIR GRIFFIN enters from one of the rooms upstairs, moves across the landing and comes down the stairs. She is carrying a number of unframed original canvases which she leans against another pile of paintings that have already been deposited in the room. She is thirty-five years old but looks much younger with the slim body of a teenager. She wears no makeup and is casually dressed in jeans and a sweater which further contributes to her apparently artless look of the classic waif child-woman. Everything she does has a graceful, feminine delicacy and she exudes an aura of vulnerable fragility. When she speaks, her voice is well modulated with no trace of a regional accent and her words are well chosen. In the distance, we hear a car approaching. She moves to window, looks out, picks up a pair of binoculars, moves out onto the outer deck, puts binoculars to eyes, picks up car approaching along coast road. She then sweeps binoculars over terrain down and to her left, obviously trying to locate something. She appears to have found it, refocuses binoculars, stares through them for a moment or two, moves inside, deposits binoculars, exits to kitchen. We hear the car come to a halt outside and the motor turn off as she re-enters carrying a cheeseboard containing some large slabs of cheese, bread, and some fruit. In her other hand she carries a long, glinting, pointed, kitchen knife. She deposits cheeseboard on table, and then, her face expressionless, plunges knife into cheese where it remains in the upright position providing a subtle, ominous accent in the foreground of the scene. The music tape has finished. She turns as the front door opens and MORGAN RICHARDS, an attractive man in his mid-forties, enters. The two regard each other for a moment, a definite tension between them.*

BLAIR. (*finally*) Hello, Morgan.

MORGAN. Hello.

BLAIR. Where did you get the station wagon?

MORGAN. Rented it in Boston. Everytime I drive this road I feel like I'm taking my life in my hands.

BLAIR. Last time. (*He nods.*)

MORGAN. How long you been up here?

BLAIR. A few days. How are the children?

MORGAN. Just fine. They send their love. (*She nods. A small pause as he studies her with a certain curious detachment.*) You're incredible. Nothing shows.

BLAIR. What?

MORGAN. Your face. After everything we've been through — nothing shows on your face.

BLAIR. The scars are internal, Morgan. (*She turns away, indicates cheeseboard.*) I thought you might be hungry.

MORGAN. Thanks but I don't have time. I'm booked back on the six o'clock ferry. (*He moves to look through canvasses.*)

BLAIR. The rest are up in the studio. I didn't know which ones you wanted.

MORGAN. I doubt if I can use any of them. Most of the work I did up here was junk.

BLAIR. Where's the exhibition?

MORGAN. Washington. Just a small gallery but it's a start.

BLAIR. Towards what?

MORGAN. Respectability. (*She moves to pick up binoculars, looks through window.*)

BLAIR. (*mildly*) Your career didn't exactly suffer because of our marriage, Morgan.

MORGAN. Appearing in the Fun Couple section of People magazine was hardly my goal when I decided to be an artist.

BLAIR. (*disinterested*) Sold a lot of paintings.

MORGAN. Because I was your husband.

BLAIR. What differences does it make? (*She has seen something.*) Damn! It *is* him!

MORGAN. Who?

BLAIR. Lombardi. I thought I spotted him before but I wasn't sure. (*offering binoculars*) Look, he's about two hundred yards away — under that rock.

MORGAN. Natural habitat. (*He doesn't move to take binoculars, she peers through them again.*)

BLAIR. I don't believe it!

MORGAN. (*slightly puzzled*) He's been shadowing you for fifteen years. Why are you so upset?

BLAIR. Because we made a deal!

MORGAN. What?

BLAIR. Never mind. (*as he picks up some canvasses*) I wonder if I should call the police. What do you think?

MORGAN. Blair, that is your problem. (*He exits through front door with canvasses. She thinks for a moment, makes a decision, moves to window or out onto deck, waves her arms, and then makes a signalling motion for LOMBARDI to come in. MORGAN reenters from outside, stops in some surprise as he sees what BLAIR is doing. She steps back into room.*) What are you doing?

BLAIR. Signalling Lombardi to come in. (*as he stares at her*) Look, I just decided that, rather than dragging the police into this, it would be better to calmly discuss it with him. I'm sure he'll be reasonable.

MORGAN. How do you know that? Have you ever talked to him before?

BLAIR. Just once. He's not quite the creep you've always made him out to be.

Morgan. (*shrugs*) It's your life. (*He starts up the stairs.*)

Blair. Morgan? (*He turns.*) I know he's harmless but I'd feel more comfortable if you stayed until he leaves.

Morgan. As long as it doesn't take longer than five minutes. And don't expect me to talk to him. (*He moves upstairs and exits into studio. BLAIR glances out of window once more, moves to bookcase, removes about three books and pushes a concealed button. A five by three square of the floor* D.L. *slides open revealing a jacuzzi. It is important that when it is closed the grooved wooden floor completely disguises it. BLAIR moves to jacuzzi, kneels, puts her hand in to test water as MORGAN, carrying some canvasses, comes out onto landing and descends stairs. He stops as he sees jacuzzi.*) What the hell is that?

Blair. Jacuzzi. I was just checking the water level. Sometimes it evaporates.

Morgan. A jacuzzi? I thought you despised anything that smacked of faddism.

Blair. In California it's a fad. Here it's an eccentricity. (*drily*) Much easier to live with. (*MORGAN moves to deposit canvasses.*)

Morgan. How long do you plan on staying?

Blair. Oh, as long as it takes to regain—some inner serenity. As it were. (*She presses button and the jacuzzi top slides back, concealing it once more.*) That's one of the reasons I had this put in. I plan to soak in warm water, gaze at the stars and replay the tapes of my life.

Morgan. Have you decided where you're going to live yet?

Blair. Not really.

Morgan. Why don't you try New York? (*as she looks*

at him) They only have nine celebrities there so they have to write about them all the time.

BLAIR. (*evenly*) Oh, I don't know. All that jostling for the spotlight seems rather undignified at my age.

MORGAN. At your age?

BLAIR. I am in imminent danger of becoming the oldest living waif since Peter Pan. (*This elicits a small smile. He turns, starts up stairs, stops, turns.*)

MORGAN. Blair, I appreciated the way you acted about the divorce.

BLAIR. (*a statement of fact*) I had no other choice.

MORGAN. I know. I appreciate it anyway.

(*He breaks eye contact, moves upstairs and exits to studio. BLAIR moves into kitchen and we can see her taking coffee from stove, putting it on tray, etc., through following. TONY LOMBARDI enters through open front door. He is a seedy, thirty-four with an intense, kinetic energy that is manifested by both his physical movements and nervous verbal style. He is wearing shabby New York street garb and carries a canvas bag that presumably contains his cameras and film. He takes in the room, dumps his bag, moves quickly around, examining room. He notices cheeseboard, moves to it, stares at knife for a moment, looks around, takes knife from cheese, looks at it for a moment, tests sharpness of blade, slides it down inside his boot, covers handle with the pant leg of his jeans. His hands are wet with excitement and he wipes them on the sides of his jeans. He moves to check front door lock and then moves to examine one of the dolls. BLAIR, a tray containing coffee pot and mugs in her hands, enters, stops as she sees him. He reaches out to pick up doll.*)

BLAIR. (*firmly*) Don't touch that! (*He wheels around and they stare at one another. Her attitude is one of calm wariness. He is extremely tense.*)

TONY. Feels weird to be on the *inside*, you know.

BLAIR. I thought we had an understanding. (*He is staring at her intensely.*)

TONY. I saw the painter drive up. Where is he — upstairs? (*BLAIR moves to put tray down.*)

BLAIR. Yes, listening to every word we say — and I'd better warn you, he's a lot less patient than I am. (*TONY abruptly starts moving around room.*)

TONY. Nice — nice. I always liked your taste. Pure class. (*indicating chair*) Is that new?

BLAIR. I thought we agreed this place was off limits.

TONY. (*still moving*) Yeah — well, extenuating circumstances.

BLAIR. What?

TONY. Poverty. Ha-ha. I mean let's not kid around here — our career is about one step away from TV game shows.

BLAIR. Our career?

TONY. I think of us as partners. You don't work — I don't work. (*He turns to stare at her.*) Jesus, this is weird — really weird — we're talking to each other. I talk and then you talk — just like a regular conversation. Weird.

BLAIR. Look, would you please not stare at me like that? It's very disconcerting.

TONY. It's like seeing you naked.

BLAIR. What?

TONY. (*He mimes camera.*) No camera between us. It's making me nervous.

BLAIR. It's making *you* nervous?

TONY. I'm sweating. (*extends hands*) Will you look at that?

BLAIR. Would you like a cup of coffee?

TONY. Coffee. Having coffee with Blair Griffin. Yeah, yeah, I'll have a cup of coffee. (*He starts to advance towards her. She speaks a trifle too intensely.*)

BLAIR. No — just — just stay over there. I'll bring it to you.

(*MORGAN comes out onto landing carrying some canvasses. TONY's head spins to look up at him.*)

MORGAN. You okay?

BLAIR. Yes. (*TONY watches him as he puts canvasses on landing, exits into studio. He wipes his hands on the side of his jeans.*) Look, Tony, we have to resolve this situation. (*notices his expression*) What is it?

TONY. First name. First time.

BLAIR. Yes. Well — now frankly, I've never understood your fixation about my career but right now it's especially baffling. I'm not in the least bit newsworthy and as a working paparazzi —

TONY. Paparazzi? Don't call me that! I'm a lot more than a paparazzi!

BLAIR. (*shrugs*) Photo-journalist — however you think of yourself.

TONY. I *think* of myself as an *historian*. (*She looks at him with amused surprise.*) That's funny? I made a joke?

BLAIR. It's just that I never thought of you that way.

TONY. How did you think of me?

BLAIR. As a pest. (*He stares at her for a moment, unsmiling.*)

TONY. (*finally*) That's okay—I have a sense of humor. I can enjoy a laugh. (*She puts his coffee on table near him.*)

BLAIR. I'm sorry—I wasn't laughing at you. I was just amused at the idea that anyone would be interested in *my* history. (*He starts moving around again.*)

TONY. You leave that to me. I've helped before—I can help again.

BLAIR. (*curiously*) Why someone like me?

TONY. Like you?

BLAIR. (*self-mocking*) Famous for being famous. Anyway, there are dozens of actresses much better known and certainly more talented. (*He wheels to face her.*)

TONY. Talented? I'm not interested in your *talent*! I'm not a *fan*, for God's sake. Jesus, that's not what I like about you.

BLAIR. Then what is it?

TONY. Your life. I like your life. (*She stares at him.*)

BLAIR. My life?

TONY. (*intensely*) Sure—*that's* the work of Art—your *life*. Why do you think I've stuck with you all these years? Right from the beginning I had this feeling we'd have an interesting life together. (*He starts moving again.*) Well, so far it hasn't been too shabby, has it? Interesting—interesting. We can't complain—we can't complain.

BLAIR. You keep saying "we."

TONY. Why not? (*He faces her.*) For the past fifteen years we've had exactly the same life. *Exactly.* Only difference is you were on the inside—I was on the outside. (*He starts prowling again.*) Restaurants, hotels, sound stages—Spain, Greece, Germany—all over the world—we were always together. (*He has stopped in front of a pair of small, silver candlesticks.*) Hey, these are great. I always liked these. What's his name—the politician—

Stevenson — he gave them to you, right? (*He starts moving again.*) I mean, take this place — I was here when you bought it. Both your weddings — funerals. Listen, even when you had your kids — I was there. Well, that's when I got that great shot of you in labor.

BLAIR. (*drily*) Yes — I never had a chance to thank you for that.

TONY. Made every wire service in the world. Hey, listen, I don't usually talk this much. It's the *situation*, you know. (*There's a fairly loud thump from upstairs.*) Jesus, what's that?

BLAIR. Morgan.

TONY. Yeah, yeah — I'm jumpy. (*MORGAN comes out onto the landing again with more canvasses. TONY doesn't take his eyes from him.*)

BLAIR. Look, would you agree to go away if I posed for a few shots?

TONY. I'm not a *portrait* photographer. (*He watches MORGAN exit again.*) Anyway, the key element would be missing.

BLAIR. What's that? (*He turns to look at her.*)

TONY. (*slowly — as if thinking it out*) It's the hunt. The tracking — the chase — the moving target — and — (*He mimes camera.*) Click — the kill . . . (*a beat*) Yeah, that's it.

BLAIR. Yes, well, I don't like being the prey anymore. I'm not sure I ever did.

TONY. Oh, come on — I beg your pardon — but come on. You used to love the camera. Of course you were just a kid then. Know the first shot I ever got of you?

BLAIR. Your coffee is getting cold.

TONY. No, this is interesting. January, 1968. Total accident. I was staked out at the Pierre trying to get a shot of, you know, the comic — he was big stuff then. Two-thirty a.m. he comes out of the side entrance with you on his arm. When the flash goes off he jumps like he's been hit with an M-1. (*He has been playing with the stereo controls and suddenly the music blares. He jumps.*) Oops — sorry. Great sound. (*He clicks it off.*) Where was I? Oh, yeah. So I didn't know what I had until he offers me five hundred for the film. Bingo — the dude is married! I mean, I was just a dumb kid in those days but not *that* dumb. So I take off — son of a bitch chases me right over to Madison. Is he kidding — no contest. Next day, on a hunch, I follow him to Vegas — you show up and we're all over the front pages. Why'd you marry him?

BLAIR. I loved him.

TONY. Yeah, well I could see it was a good *career* move, Blair — (*She reacts to the use of her name.*) — but not who I would have picked for you at all. Not at all.

BLAIR. You didn't know him.

TONY. Know him? He used to beat you up. I got a trunkful of shots.

BLAIR. He drank, Tony.

TONY. Yeah, drank himself to death — (*points out of window*) Right over that cliff — ha-ha. Sorry, but I hated the son of a bitch.

BLAIR. I know. (*MORGAN comes out onto the landing.*) Sit down and drink your coffee, Tony. (*He sits.*) You take it black?

TONY. Yeah, black. Always black. (*MORGAN, carrying a large canvas of a portrait of BLAIR in front of him, comes down stairs.*)

MORGAN. Look, I don't care if you keep this but I thought the kids might like to have it in their room. (*TONY has risen and is moving towards him.*)

TONY. Hi, I'm Tony Lombardi. We've never met formally.

(*We see the glint of the knife as he plunges it through BLAIR's face on the canvas and into MORGAN's stomach. MORGAN's face assumes an unbelieving expression before his mouth gapes open. TONY withdraws the bloody knife and blood starts seeping through the slit created on BLAIR's face in the canvas. MORGAN looks down, and slowly crumples to the floor, the bloody canvas over him as TONY moves to one side of the stage, kneels, and starts to retch. BLAIR, her eyes enormous, starts to scream and scream as the lights blackout. An echo microphone picks up her screams and they reverberate through the theatre for some time after the blackout.*)

CURTAIN

End of Act One, Scene 1

SCENE 2

THE TIME: *Two hours later.*

AT RISE: *Some lights have been turned on and the body of MORGAN has been removed, but, apart from this, the set should look the same as we saw it last. The only exception is that the two small, silver candlesticks have been removed but we shouldn't notice this. A uniformed policewoman, Sergeant DORIS AYLESWORTH, a pleasant looking, appealing woman in her mid thirties, is sitting at the table writing in a notepad. The front door opens and Lieutenant GUS BRADEN, wearing rumpled, old fishing clothes, enters. He is a flawed, idiosyncratic,*

*physical wreck of a man probably in his early fifties
with an attractive, likable, lived-in face. He has
managed to survive his considerable private wars
with his sense of humor intact. He is also nobody's
fool. He stops, takes in room.*

DORIS. Where the hell were you?

GUS. Out in the boat.

DORIS. Can never find a cop when you need one.

GUS. Where's the tootsie?

DORIS. Upstairs, waiting for you.

GUS. When did it happen?

DORIS. Couple of hours ago. They fill you in?

GUS. (*nods*) Old Bert Radcliff was waiting for me on
the dock. (*as he divests himself of battered parka*) Spas-
tically hopping up and down with the eyes of a demented
chameleon. Haven't had so much excitement in this em-
balmed little community since that whale washed ashore
—(*He puts jacket on chair.*)—and the Mayor's dachs-
hund tried to hump it. What else you know?

DORIS. Just about everything. We know who did it
and how. The only thing we don't know is why. (*He
starts to amble around, leisurely examining the room.*)

GUS. That's the psychologist's racket, not ours. Body
at the morgue? (*She nods.*) Where exactly did he croak?

DORIS. "Croak"? He was stabbed in the stomach. (*indicating*) Right there.

GUS. How'd she get away?

DORIS. Guy started to throw up—not your cold-
blooded killer type—she ran out, got in the station
wagon and drove to—

GUS. She had the keys with her?

DORIS. Keys were in the car. Husband had rented it in
Boston. Hertz—I checked. (*He gives her a sardonic look*

of approval.) Anyway, she drove to the phone on high-way three, called the station and asked for you.

GUS. By name?

DORIS. Of course by name. What else — by footprint? (*He resumes his examination of room.*)

GUS. I'm just surprised she remembered me. We only met once and that was four years ago.

DORIS. (*drily*) Well you must have been especially "colorful" that day. (*He looks at her.*) Where was it?

GUS. On some TV talk show. I was hawking my book and she was beating the drum for some movie. You get a good description of the punk — Lombardi?

DORIS. Down to the pimple on his neck. She must have a photographic memory. (*He looks up at beams.*)

GUS. Those beams real?

DORIS. No — hollow.

GUS. My God, a family of four could live in there. (*He starts to climb up.*)

DORIS. Sure, that's a great way to put your back out again. (*He stops.*) We've searched the place top to bottom, Gus. He's long gone but with that description it's only a matter of time before we pick him up.

GUS. (*coming down*) He take anything?

DORIS. The husband's wallet, watch, and ring.

GUS. Anything else missing?

DORIS. She didn't think so. She seemed a bit vague about that.

GUS. What else she tell you?

DORIS. That's about it. I think she was waiting to talk to you.

GUS. She say why?

DORIS. She didn't have to. (*She shrugs.*) She's a movie star. They're not used to talking to the common people.

GUS. Can't get much more hoi polloi than me, kid.

DORIS. Yeah, but you're famous.

GUS. Semi-famous. And very ex.

DORIS. But you still have all the celebrity qualifications. (*He looks at her.*) You appeared on the Phil Donahue Show. God knows, I've had to watch the video tape enough times.

GUS. (*wryly*) Doris, we've known each other for too long.

DORIS. You want me to call her down?

GUS. Give me a couple of minutes to look around. (*He stands, looks around; with some vehemence:*) Jesus, I *hate* all this!

DORIS. What?

GUS. Crime!

DORIS. You're a *cop*, for God's sake!

GUS. Yeah, well I came here to get away from all that mephitic garbage. It just gets me down, you know. (*indicating notes*) What are those?

DORIS. Oh, I had some time to kill so I just jotted down some notes on her background. You want to read them?

GUS. Read them to me. Just give me the highlights. (*He continues to amble slowly around room as DORIS consults notes.*)

DORIS. Don't know where she came from originally. Started working as a model in New York when she was eighteen. Print stuff mostly — made all the covers. Went into acting — did some off-Broadway show.

GUS. "The Seagull."

DORIS. (*surprised*) How did you know that?

GUS. I saw it.

DORIS. La de da.

GUS. (*examining front door*) You notice this door has been forced?

DORIS. (*sarcastically*) Wow, you don't miss a trick, do you? (*She goes back to notes.*) About that time she got mixed up with Jerry Pavan.

GUS. The comic? (*He takes out cigarette holder, inserts cigarette through following.*)

DORIS. Yeah. He was married at the time. She followed him to Vegas, he divorced his wife, married her, put her in his next movie. She became a star—he went back to playing saloons. From all reports the marriage was pretty stormy. He drank and—(*She automatically holds out lighter. He bends to light cigarette in holder. She regards holder.*) That cigarette holder looks—

GUS. I believe incongruous is the word you're searching for.

DORIS. No, that's not the word. You smell of fish.

GUS. Beer. I told you—I was out in the boat.

DORIS. Yeah, you two are a matched pair. You both need your barnacles scraped and a new paint job.

GUS. (*looking around*) I know—I know—disgrace to the force.

DORIS. You don't even carry a weapon anymore.

GUS. Sorry, sir. The only time I've fired it in ten years is to start the three-legged race at the Kiwanis picnic. What happened to him?

DORIS. Jerry Pavan? (*He nods.*) He was killed in that car accident ten years ago. Went over the cliff at Randall's Point. (*He moves to look out window.*) Wasn't the first time it's happened—or the last for that matter. They still haven't fixed the damned road.

GUS. Were you here then?

DORIS. Yeah, the first year on the force. I investigated the accident. (*He turns to look at her.*) He was drunk—rainy night—bad combination.

GUS. Where was she?

Doris. In the house. Saw the whole thing from that window. Had a shiner out to here—they'd had a fight and he'd taken a swing at her.

Gus. Yeah, I never found him funny either.

Doris. Don't you remember that shot of her at the graveside that made the front pages everywhere? Black veil—one tear trickling down her left cheek. Big stuff.

Gus. Who took the photo?

Doris. Tony Lombardi. I checked.

Gus. (*admiringly*) You're aces, kid.

Doris. So how come I'm not a detective?

Gus. You don't look good in a fedora. (*He moves over to examine books in shelves.*) She has my book here.

Doris. Yeah, I noticed. Weird. (*He looks at her.*) Tolstoi, Dickens, Flaubert, Stendahl, Shakespeare, Dostoevski, and—Gus Braden. It's like one of those "What's wrong with this picture?"

Gus. (*moving to another bookshelf*) I'm beginning to understand why Joe divorced you. Anyway, it's just in the wrong rack. Looks like she owns every mystery and crime book ever written. (*checking another shelf*) All the philosophers, science, poetry, drama—either she's better read than Alistair Cook—or she's giving a party and wants to impress people.

Doris. She never invites anyone here. Sort of a secret place to "get away from it all."

Gus. Not too choked up about her, are you, kid?

Doris. Not true. I was *prepared* not to like her.

Gus. What changed your mind?

Doris. Vanity. (*He doesn't understand.*) She remembered my name. It was *ten years* ago when I investigated that accident and she remembered my damn name.

Gus. Doris, you're so easy.

Doris. You should know.

(*BLAIR appears on the landing and comes down the stairs. Her manner is warm, pleasant, controlled and any sign of strain shows itself in subtle, unusual ways. GUS turns to face her and they look at one another for a moment before she speaks. At the moment he is not succumbing to her charm and during the following, for some reason, his manner is somewhat combatant.*)

BLAIR. I'm sorry to keep you waiting. I was making arrangements for the—the funeral. It's Gus, isn't it?

GUS. Yeah, Gus Braden. We met once in Boston.

BLAIR. I remember you very well. You gave me half your pastrami sandwich and you were wearing mismatched socks. (*DORIS is watching this exchange with some amusement.*)

GUS. Yes—well, I was probably nervous.

BLAIR. I found it very appealing.

GUS. Are you up to a couple of questions, Miss Griffin?

BLAIR. Please call me Blair. Look, naturally I'm still somewhat shaky but I realize a certain procedure has to be followed. Oh, I'm sorry—would you care for a drink or a cup of coffee?

GUS. Well, I wouldn't mind a—

DORIS. (*firmly*) He'll take coffee. (*as BLAIR nods and goes to make a move*) Would you like me to make it?

BLAIR. (*gratefully*) Doris, that would be a great help. (*DORIS exits. BLAIR indicates a chair.*) Please.

GUS. I'll stand. (*She sits.*) Look, this seems all very cut and dried but I have a couple of questions about Tony Lombardi.

BLAIR. I don't really know that much about him. I've only spoken to him once before today.

GUS. When was that?

BLAIR. About two months ago. In a Los Angeles court-house.

GUS. How come?

BLAIR. Well, Lombardi was always a nuisance but, over the years, I had become used to him—rather like a rarely glimpsed mole—well, wart, I suppose. Then about six months ago he started to become really intrusive—tried to get a shot of my children at school, interrupted a difficult take on a movie so I—excuse me, are you cold? I suddenly feel very chilly. Do you mind if I light a fire? (*She gets up, moves to fireplace, proceeds to get log from container through following.*) So I decided to take him to court for harassment—invasion of privacy. On the morning that the case was going to come to trial he accosted me in the corridor of the courthouse—(*She is having difficulty with log.*)

GUS. You want some help?

BLAIR. No, it's all right. (*She smiles.*) I'm as tough as nails. (*She dumps log on fire.*) Don't be fooled by the way I look.

GUS. (*matter of factly*) I'm not. (*She turns to look at him.*)

BLAIR. Really? Most people think of me as being rather frail.

GUS. (*laconically*) That so? (*a small pause*)

BLAIR. What is it, Lieutenant? Did you once have a bad experience with an actress—or did you just see one of my movies? (*He doesn't respond to her amused tone, moves away.*)

GUS. What did Lombardi say to you?

BLAIR. He pleaded with me to drop the charges and—well, I started to feel sorry for him.

GUS. So the case never came to trial?

BLAIR. No. Lombardi promised to abide by certain

conditions I laid out and I believed him. One was that this place was off limits. When I spotted him here I decided that, rather than bothering you, I'd invite him in and talk to him. (*He turns to look at her.*)

GUS. You invited him in?

BLAIR. Didn't I tell the police that? What is it?

GUS. I was just wondering why the door was forced.

BLAIR. What?

GUS. The front door lock has been forced.

BLAIR. Oh, that was me. (*He looks questioningly at her.*) When I arrived here I found I'd forgotten my key so I jimmied the lock. (*He moves to examine lock.*)

GUS. Pretty professional job.

BLAIR. I've been in three caper movies. Give me the right tools and I can even crack a safe. (*He looks at her for a second, opens the door, looks out.*)

GUS. Is that gate the only entrance to the grounds?

BLAIR. Yes. The house is set on a promontory.

GUS. What about the cliffs coming up from the beach? Could anyone scale them?

BLAIR. Not unless they were Edmund Hillary.

GUS. Yeah — well from what I hear this guy Lombardi can get in anywhere he wants.

BLAIR. He's ingenious, Lieutenant — not a magician.

GUS. Use that bolt tonight.

BLAIR. If you insist.

GUS. Look, lady, it's your life but right now I'm responsible for it. (*DORIS enters from kitchen with tray and moves to deposit it on coffee table.*)

BLAIR. Oh, thank you, Doris. (*BLAIR moves to pour coffee through following.*) You take cream?

DORIS. Nothing for me, thanks. (*checking watch*) I have to get going.

BLAIR. Anxious to get back to your kids?

DORIS. No. I mean they're visiting with my ex-husband in L.A. (*BLAIR gives GUS coffee.*)

BLAIR. Do you think you'll catch Lombardi?

GUS. (*shrugs*) There are only three ways off this island — by plane, by ferry, or by charter boat. If he tries any of them we'll pick him up.

DORIS. Especially since your description is so accurate.

BLAIR. (*remembering*) Oh, I can do better than that. When I was upstairs I remembered I had a photo of him. (*She takes it out of her pocket.*) It's a trifle grainy but — well, here. (*She hands it to GUS and he and DORIS look at it.*) It was taken on a telephoto lens — in Spain, I think. We were staying with the Dalis.

GUS. What Dalis?

BLAIR. (*evenly*) The Salvador Dalis.

GUS. (*drily*) Oh, *those* Dalis.

BLAIR. One day I was bored, saw him outside, as usual, and clicked off a few shots.

GUS. I take it we can have this.

BLAIR. Of course.

GUS. Doris, you'd better drive this in and run off some copies we can circulate. (*She nods, heads for door.*)

DORIS. You want me to come back to pick you up?

GUS. No, it's okay. I have the Jeep.

DORIS. See you later.

BLAIR. Goodbye, Doris. Thank you for your help. (*DORIS nods and exits. BLAIR looks after her; simply.*) Doris has the gift of compassion. I always find it very touching when total strangers are kind to me.

GUS. Yeah — she's a good kid. (*BLAIR leans forward, speaks conspiratorially.*)

BLAIR. And now that she's gone — would you like a drink? (*a small pause*)

GUS. (*unsmiling*) You don't miss much, do you?

BLAIR. I thought it might relax you.

GUS. Are you trying to get in my good graces?

BLAIR. Absolutely. (*He still doesn't respond.*)

GUS. (*with some ambiguity*) That's what I like — a woman without guile.

BLAIR. (*indicating bar*) Help yourself, Gus. (*He moves to the bar, pours himself drink through following.*)

GUS. By the way, how do you do that? Remember people's monikers?

BLAIR. Oh, I'm afraid that's just a trick a politician — I think it was George McGovern — taught me. It's all by association. (*She sits.*) Sometimes it can backfire though. I was once at an opening night and found myself in the lobby crushed next to a producer I knew. Very proud of myself I came up with the name of his wife and said, "And how's Sharon?" He said, "I lost her, Blair." Well, I quickly adjusted my face and said, "I know — I heard about that. I was so sorry. I wrote you a condolence note but you probably haven't received it yet." The man looked at me as if I was crazy and said, "I mean I've lost her here — in the crowd — I can't find her." (*She doesn't smile but looks puzzled.*) What an odd time to think of that story. I've just lost my husband and I tell you that story. Am I cracking up?

GUS. (*dry as dust*) You've had a bad day.

BLAIR. And as you're saying that you're looking at me in a very peculiar manner. (*He doesn't say anything.*) What are you thinking, Lieutenant? Come on, you can tell me.

GUS. (*flatly*) I'm thinking I haven't seen this much control since Whitey Ford.

BLAIR. Are you saying that I'm unfeeling? (*He shrugs. Angrily:*) That's a gigantic assumption, Lieutenant!

GUS. (*unimpressed*) Are we having our first fight?

BLAIR. How can you possibly know what I'm experiencing right now?

GUS. Look, lady, you *asked* me. Now you've just seen your husband stabbed to death and you're sitting around pouring coffee and telling cute stories. What should I think?

BLAIR. Would you feel better if my eyes brimmed every time I mentioned Morgan's name?

GUS. No, but you might. (*She regains control, looks at him for a moment.*)

BLAIR. Do you have some sort of aversion to meeting film stars? Is that it?

GUS. No — but I'm not going to have an emotional hemorrhage over it, either. (*She looks at him for a moment, nods.*)

BLAIR. Yes — well, I'd better light that fire. (*She moves away to look for matches, her back to him.*) That's funny, I can't seem to find the taper matches. I usually keep them behind this box of Morgan's sketch pencils but — (*She stops and suddenly her shoulders start to convulsively shudder.*)

GUS. What is it? (*She just shakes her head, her back still to him.*) What's the matter?

BLAIR. I — I don't know. All of a sudden — something hit me in the middle of — of my chest and — (*She turns to face him. Her face is wet and tears are literally streaming down her cheeks. He stares at her for a moment, completely nonplussed.*)

GUS. (*embarrassed*) Look, I'm sorry. It was stupid of me to — can I get you a — a glass of water or anything? (*Her expression changes and she speaks in a crisp, totally controlled voice.*)

BLAIR. No thank you. All right, that was the full flood. I could also give you one single tear coursing down my left cheek, two slow tears on the right, or perhaps the more subtle moist eyes. (*He is staring at her unbelievingly.*) Now, does that make you feel better? (*He watches her as she moves to get kleenex, blots her face.*) The first thing that an actress learns to do is cry, Lieutenant. And you know why? It's so *easy.* Very effective but the cheapest trick in the book. Have I made my point? (*He is angry at being taken in but tries not to show it.*)

GUS. What point?

BLAIR. That tears are the appearance of emotion, not emotion itself. I stopped using them as emotional currency a long time ago.

GUS. (*sourly*) Yeah, well that must save you a lot on mascara bills.

BLAIR. Look, I wasn't trying to make you look foolish. I was just showing you that anyone can cry. I can do it on cue and I'm a *terrible* actress.

GUS. I wouldn't say that.

BLAIR. It's all right. I know my career is based on bone structure. (*She moves away to fire.*)

GUS. A little more than that I think.

BLAIR. Luck?

GUS. You got a great keester.

BLAIR. What?

GUS. Derriere.

BLAIR. You'll just say anything that pops into your head, won't you?

GUS. Look, you were fishing and in my quaint way I was trying to respond by saying maybe you were successful because of sex appeal.

BLAIR. Nobody's ever accused me of being sexy. (*drily*) At least not in public. (*They look at one another for a moment.*)

GUS. Anything else I should know? (*a small pause*)

BLAIR. Yes, there is something else. (*She turns away, proceeds to strike match to light fire.*) You'll find out sooner or later so I may as well tell you now. (*a beat*) I had a great affection for Morgan—I always will, but any—intense emotional connection ended some months ago. (*The flame on the match goes out. She strikes another during following.*) We were in the process of getting a divorce—it was to become final next week. That's why I asked him here—to pick up his paintings. (*The match goes out again.*) Damn. (*She lights another through following.*)

GUS. Cleaning house?

BLAIR. In a way.

GUS. Bad feelings?

BLAIR. You ever been divorced?

GUS. Yes.

BLAIR. Then you know that, despite what anyone says, no divorce is *completely* amicable. But we—(*She stops.*) I—I can't seem to keep this match alight.

GUS. And I wouldn't attempt any brain surgery for a while. Your hand is shaking to beat the band.

BLAIR. Oh dear, how embarrassing after that brave speech I made about being so tough. (*His attitude softens slightly.*)

GUS. (*gruffly*) Here, let me do it. (*He takes matches, kneels, lights fire through following as she picks up his empty glass, replenishes his drink.*)

BLAIR. Anyway, we had survived the storm and ended up—well, not friends but on our *way* to friendship.

GUS. How about legally?

BLAIR. Legally? Oh, I see what you mean. (*She hands him drink; he sits.*) No, I don't believe in alimony so that was no problem. (*curiously*) Look, do you mind if I ask *you* a question?

GUS. Sure.

BLAIR. Are you wearing odd socks *now*? (*For the second time we see him thrown off balance.*)

GUS. (*sheepishly*) I always do. (*He responds to her amused, quizzical expression, awkwardly.*) It started as a mistake, became a superstition and then—an affectation.

BLAIR. When did it become a superstition?

GUS. (*embarrassed*) I was wearing them the day my book made the New York Times' best seller list.

BLAIR. Well, Gus—now that I've discovered you're as eccentric and human as everyone else, why don't you drop the hard-nosed cop act for a while? (*He regards her for a moment but is not ready to take the bait yet.*)

GUS. Yeah, well I just have a couple more questions and I'll be out of your hair. (*He rises, inserts cigarette in holder, moves to coat to get matches.*) Can you think of any reason Lombardi would want to kill your husband?

BLAIR. No. But then I can't think of a reason why anyone would want to kill anyone. Can you?

GUS. Sure—five. (*as she looks at him*) There are five reasons why most people murder: money, revenge, love, jealousy and fear. There are some sub-headings.

BLAIR. Sub-headings?

GUS. Sure. For instance, under fear there would be blackmail. You dig?

BLAIR. Blackmail? How can anyone be blackmailed today? I mean today every pecadillo seems to be totally acceptable in the prevailing morality.

GUS. What about if the person is in the public eye?

BLAIR. Especially if the person is in the public eye. (*She shrugs.*) Look, the fact of the matter is that the American public will accept anything—except being bored. (*He lights his cigarette.*)

GUS. Do you think Lombardi was jealous? (*She thinks for a moment.*)

BLAIR. Yes. Well, I suppose possessive would be a more accurate word. Of course, there was no logical reason for that but then jealousy is always illogical, isn't it? Mind you, I still don't understand why anyone could kill out of jealousy, do you?

GUS. Yes. (*a small pause*)

BLAIR. Professionally speaking?

GUS. What else?

BLAIR. You sounded as if you once came close. (*another pause*)

GUS. No, I didn't.

BLAIR. I sensed that.

GUS. (*finally*) What are you — a witch?

BLAIR. No, just highly intuitive. (*They look at one another for a moment before he suddenly tenses.*) What is — (*He quickly puts his hand out so that it covers her mouth. He listens for a second.*)

GUS. Look, I don't want you to panic. Just get down on the floor and stay there. (*He removes his hand from her mouth.*)

BLAIR. What?

GUS. Get on the floor and don't move. There's someone outside. (*She sinks to the floor, curls up by the side of the couch. He moves towards light switches.*)

BLAIR. How do you know?

GUS. I heard him! (*He hits switches, reducing the room to semi-darkness.*)

BLAIR. It could be one of your police —

GUS. No. Keep quiet and don't move. (*We see him fumble inside his jacket.*) Damn.

BLAIR. What?

GUS. I don't have a weapon. You have a flashlight?

BLAIR. On the counter top. (*He quickly moves to counter, picks up flashlight, shines it up onto skylight.*)

GUS. Can anyone get in through the skylight?

BLAIR. No way.

GUS. Kitchen door?

BLAIR. It's locked.

GUS. Okay—sit tight. (*He turns off flashlight, moves to front door, flattens himself against wall. We hear a fist gently rapping against front door. Three times. Silence.*) Stay where you are. (*We hear the rapping again. Twice. Silence. A pause.*)

BLAIR. Is he still there?

GUS. I'm not sure. He may be trying the kitchen door. Don't move. (*GUS exits into kitchen, disappears. A pause. The front door slowly swings wide open. A brief pause and a FIGURE enters, moves a few feet into the room, stops. Suddenly the flashlight beams through the open front door onto the FIGURE.*) Okay, just stand perfectly still and you won't get hurt. (*The FIGURE freezes.*) Now turn around very slowly. (*The FIGURE turns around and the flashlight illuminates the face of MAGGIE STRAT-TEN. GUS hits the switches and the room is illuminated. We now clearly see an extremely beautiful woman probably in her mid-forties, with a casual, friendly manner spiced by a quick wit. Right now she is in a state of emotional turmoil.*) Who the hell are you?

MAGGIE. Maggie Stratten. Are you Lieutenant Braden?

GUS. Believe it or not.

MAGGIE. The policeman said I—(*as BLAIR stands up*) Blair?

BLAIR. I'm sorry, Maggie. We thought it might be Lombardi coming back. (*The blood drains from MAGGIE's face.*)

MAGGIE. Then it's true?

BLAIR. I'm afraid so, Maggie. How did you know about it?

MAGGIE. There — there was a news flash on the TV. I was in the Boston airport. I didn't believe it at first but then — (*She trails off, drops the overnight bag she is holding to the floor, stands looking disoriented and forlorn. Finally:*) Oh — God.

BLAIR. Maggie, are you all right? (*MAGGIE just stares at her. There is a small pause before BLAIR moves to embrace her but the embrace is subtly awkward, tentative, not quite natural.*) Now, now — take it easy. (*BLAIR breaks, looks at her from arm's length.*) You all right? (*MAGGIE manages a nod.*) I'll get you a brandy. (*BLAIR moves to pour brandy.*)

GUS. You live in Boston, Miss Stratten?

MAGGIE. (*still disoriented*) What? Oh no — L.A. I'm — I'm Blair's agent — I was on my way here with a script. I was going to stay in Boston overnight but when I heard — Look, I'm sorry — I have to sit down. (*She does. BLAIR hands her the brandy.*)

BLAIR. Here, drink this. (*MAGGIE takes it but doesn't drink and seems almost unaware she is holding it.*)

MAGGIE. I was okay on the phone — I suppose I didn't truly believe it, but then the taxi driver started talking about it and when I saw the police cars outside — (*She trails off, looks at BLAIR.*) You okay? (*BLAIR makes a gesture.*) Stupid question.

BLAIR. Drink the brandy.

MAGGIE. Jesus. Why *Morgan*? What — what exactly happened?

BLAIR. Maggie, I know how you feel but I'm having rather a difficult time myself right now and I'm not really up to — (*She stops, takes a breath.*) Look, my falling apart is not going to help anyone.

MAGGIE. I understand. Maybe I shouldn't have come. It's just making things worse for you.

BLAIR. (*steadily*) Things couldn't be worse, Maggie. And I'm glad you're here. (*The phone rings. BLAIR answers it.*) Hello — Yes, it is — Well, I'm not sure. I believe there are some of his clothes upstairs — No, that's all right, I understand — Yes, I'll call you back, Mr. Metcalf. (*She hangs up.*) It's the undertaker. They need some of — of Morgan's clothes. Would you excuse me for a few minutes?

GUS. Of course. (*BLAIR moves to stairs, starts to ascend, stops, turns.*)

BLAIR. Maggie, I'd like you to stay for the funeral. (*a slight pause*)

MAGGIE. (*a tinge of gratitude*) You would?

BLAIR. Yes. If you want to.

MAGGIE. I do. (*a beat*) Thank you, Blair. (*BLAIR nods and GUS watches her as she goes upstairs and exits. He turns back as MAGGIE downs the brandy in one gulp. She looks up, sees him regarding her.*) I warn you, Lieutenant, I don't have quite as much grit as Blair. It's quite possible I'm going to go to pieces and make a fool of myself in front of you.

GUS. (*kindly*) I can take it. (*MAGGIE moves to survey bar.*)

MAGGIE. What do you think? Is getting smashed going to help?

GUS. I don't think you're going to get crocked on two brandies.

MAGGIE. Five. (*She moves to bar, pours herself another drink as GUS studies photo of BLAIR.*) I had three on the plane.

GUS. Could have fooled me.

MAGGIE. I'm an extremely predictable sort of drunk.

I'm cold sober for five drinks. Six and I'm anybody's. Seven, and my face falls into the soup. (*holds up bottle*) You want one of these, Lieutenant? (*He glances over at her.*)

GUS. Uh—no, thanks. And call me Gus. (*She proceeds to pour drink in another glass during following.*)

MAGGIE. Okay. Come to think of it, you don't look like a police detective.

GUS. What's a detective supposed to look like?

MAGGIE. Humphrey Bogart.

GUS. It's my day off. Tomorrow I'll look like Bogart.

MAGGIE. Promise? (*She hands him a drink.*) Here.

GUS. I said I didn't want one.

MAGGIE. I could tell you didn't mean it.

GUS. Jesus, what is it about me? It's like I had a sign around my neck—"Give this bum a drink before he gets the D.T.'s."

MAGGIE. Never look a gift horse in the mouth, Gus.

GUS. (*taking drink*) Or any other place for that matter. (*They silently toast before she glances at photo in his hand.*)

MAGGIE. She's really something, isn't she? (*She moves away, looks up at landing.*) Classy as Tiffany silver, grace under pressure—all that good stuff.

GUS. (*putting photo back*) She seems a—very private person.

MAGGIE. (*almost casual*) She's not what she seems. (*He turns to look at her.*)

GUS. That would be too much to hope for.

MAGGIE. You find her attractive?

GUS. Strange question.

MAGGIE. Why? A lot of men do. I've never been able to really figure it out. What *is* it?

GUS. You couldn't have asked a worse person.

MAGGIE. You're a man.

GUS. My libido's been living in a rest home for years.

MAGGIE. Memory gone too?

GUS. (*a slight shrug*) She's unique.

MAGGIE. She's not really. She's totally made up. (*GUS is watching her as she flops into chair.*)

GUS. Aren't we all?

MAGGIE. Perhaps. But the difference with Blair is that it's all very calculated. She's like a human computer — absorbs knowledge from every person she's ever known, stores it away, decides whether it's useful before she adds it to the patina of personality she's created. (*GUS is studying her with a mixture of extreme interest and curiosity.*)

GUS. Created?

MAGGIE. Fools most people.

GUS. She's that good an actress?

MAGGIE. (*flatly*) The best in the world — offscreen, of course.

GUS. Why not on screen?

MAGGIE. Because it's someone else's script. (*She gets up.*) Blair believes in her *own* script. That's one of the reasons she's the consummate con artist. (*She moves to look into fire.*)

GUS. What are the other reasons? (*She turns to look at him; thinks for a moment.*)

MAGGIE. She's a genius at using — sometimes creating — synchronicity. She can take a combination of events, orchestrate them, and make it all work for her.

GUS. (*drily*) How long have you two been best buddies?

MAGGIE. (*shrugs*) I'm her agent. I don't have to like her. Out of self-protection I try to understand her.

GUS. Is she ambitious?

MAGGIE. No more than Eva Peron. That's why she only attaches herself to men of achievement.

GUS. What are you trying to say here, Maggie? That she's slept her way to the top?

MAGGIE. Of course not. Just the middle. Sorry, bitchy thing to say.

GUS. Would she commit murder to get what she wants? (*MAGGIE looks at him, doesn't answer.*) Protect what she has?

MAGGIE. You think she had something to do with Morgan's death?

GUS. I'm just trying to get a character sketch. I like to know who I'm dealing with.

MAGGIE. Oh, what the hell — I think I'll have one more of these. (*She moves to bar to pour drink.*)

GUS. You haven't answered me.

MAGGIE. Loaded question.

GUS. Not really. Most people are capable of committing murder — in the heat of the moment.

MAGGIE. Blair never does anything in the heat of the moment.

GUS. Do *you* think she had anything to do with Morgan's death? (*a pause*)

MAGGIE. (*finally; almost regretfully*) No.

GUS. Why not?

MAGGIE. She had absolutely nothing to gain. (*She looks at him for a moment.*) You know, I must be getting drunk — you're beginning to look more like Bogart.

GUS. Funny what drink can do to you. (*puzzled*) You're beginning to look familiar too.

MAGGIE. What time do you usually go to bed?

GUS. (*puzzled*) Two or three in the morning. I don't sleep well.

MAGGIE. Then, that's it. Think of me in black and white without a nose job.

GUS. The late, late show.

MAGGIE. All purpose second woman — attractive, but not too attractive — never got the guy, best friend of leading lady — the female Ralph Bellamy.

GUS. You were very good.

MAGGIE. And halfway down a one-way street to mother parts.

GUS. You quit?

MAGGIE. Look, the only way to be in Hollywood is twenty-three, gorgeous and a star — *or* a very rich, very powerful, very short agent. Took me a while but I'm real hot stuff out there, kid. (*She drifts away, looks at painting.*)

GUS. How long you been handling Blair?

MAGGIE. About a year. (*a shrug*) I needed a challenge. (*She looks at another painting.*) That man *could* paint, couldn't he? (*GUS is watching her. Her voice gets a little tighter.*) Was it — fast, Gus?

GUS. Real quick. (*She nods.*) What was he like?

MAGGIE. (*still looking at painting*) Morgan? Oh — nothing special when you first met him — handsome but — reserved — shy, really. Very — kind. Never did one thing I know to — (*Her voice starts to crack.*) — ever hurt anyone in — (*Tears have welled up in her eyes.*) Oh, shit! It's just that there are so many s-o-b's who — I'm sorry — I seem to be disintegrating here — must have been that sixth brandy — is my mascara running? Look, do you have anything I can — (*He gives her a handkerchief.*)

GUS. Here. (*She dries her face.*)

MAGGIE. Damndest — thing. I usually never cry before three a.m.

GUS. I won't tell anyone if you won't.

MAGGIE. Smells of fish.

GUS. You want nice, go cry with a decorator. (*She has regained some control, expels a sigh.*)

MAGGIE. Well, I'd better get into town and check in somewhere. Where's the best place to stay?

GUS. I'll take care of it. (*He moves to phone, studies it.*) What the hell is this?

MAGGIE. Speaker phone. Blair always likes to do two things at once. Here. (*She puts receiver on cradle and GUS dials number. As he pushes the buttons the dial tones are quite audible through the speaker.*)

WOMAN'S VOICE. (*on speaker*) Harbor House.

GUS. Alice? It's Gus.

WOMAN'S VOICE. (*on speaker*) How you doing, Gus? Did that ointment I told you about help the hemorrhoids?

GUS. (*drily*) Yeah, don't know what I'd do without you, Alice. Listen, do you have a room available? It's for a friend of mine named Maggie Stratten.

WOMAN'S VOICE. (*on speaker*) Sure, we'll take care of her.

GUS. She'll be there in fifteen minutes. Thanks, Alice. (*He clicks off phone, turns to MAGGIE.*) One of the guys will run you in. Tell them I said so.

MAGGIE. Thanks, Gus. (*She picks up bag, moves to door, turns.*) By the way—I quite like the smell of fish. (*He nods, she exits. He drifts over to a chess game, studies a game that is in progress. BLAIR enters, stops on landing. She has changed into a house robe.*)

BLAIR. You play?

GUS. Not anymore.

BLAIR. Wealth of subtext there.

GUS. Not what you'd imagine. I used to play with my son. Who were you playing with? (*She descends stairs.*)

BLAIR. Bobby Fischer. We play by mail.

GUS. Who wins?

BLAIR. He does. Most of the time.

GUS. You only know famous people?

BLAIR. Is that a crime?

GUS. No, but highly suspect — like men who wear leather pants. (*She moves to put another log on the fire.*)

BLAIR. Should my ears be red?

GUS. Your name did come up.

BLAIR. What did she say?

GUS. Nothing much. (*She turns to look at him.*)

BLAIR. That bad, huh?

GUS. (*shrugs*) Just girl talk.

BLAIR. It's all right, Gus. Whatever she said is perfectly understandable.

GUS. Why?

BLAIR. She was having an affair with my husband. That's the reason our marriage broke up. (*He is staring at her.*) That's why she was in Boston. She was waiting for Morgan. Didn't you wonder why she suddenly showed up?

GUS. She said she was on her way here to give you a script.

BLAIR. And you believed her?

GUS. I get real dopey around a pretty puss. They met through you?

BLAIR. Did it all to myself. I think we could use some more light in here. (*She moves to turn on some lamps during following.*)

GUS. How long has it been going on?

BLAIR. About six months. At least that's when I found out about it. (*She moves to stack canvasses through following.*)

GUS. How did you take the news?

BLAIR. The affair? (*He nods. She shrugs.*) One can't

really blame people for how they *feel*. It's out of one's control.

GUS. Sure. And the check's in the mail.

BLAIR. (*matter-of-fact*) I'm used to people leaving me.

GUS. You're full of surprises.

BLAIR. Started with my father when I was eleven years old. (*She looks at him.*) Matter of fact, you remind me of him. (*He regards her for a long moment.*)

GUS. Swell.

BLAIR. Oh, I don't mean you look like him. He was much younger. (*He winces very slightly.*)

GUS. Even better.

BLAIR. It's more the way we — relate.

GUS. That's too recondite for me.

BLAIR. I mean the way you keep me off balance. Rather like a slugger and a good counter puncher.

GUS. Doesn't sound like the basis of a beautiful friendship, Louis.

BLAIR. But fun to watch.

GUS. There's no audience.

BLAIR. That's when I give my best performances. (*He looks at her for a moment before moving to get his coat.*) Maggie staying in town?

GUS. I arranged a room for her.

BLAIR. I suppose I should have asked her to stay here. (*He turns to look at her.*)

GUS. That would definitely have won you the Redbook hostess of the year award.

BLAIR. (*simply*) She's in a bad way. She was still in love with Morgan.

GUS. Is that why you invited her to stay for the funeral?

BLAIR. One tries not to be mean spirited on an occasion like this.

GUS. (*curiously*) Where you from originally?

BLAIR. Little town in South Carolina. Why?

GUS. You talk funny.

BLAIR. So do you. (*He reacts.*) All those cute, antiquated, slang expressions sprinkled with erudite words to make sure people get the message that you really know better. What is that all about?

GUS. I declared a moritorium on all words invented after 1950.

BLAIR. Why?

GUS. I had enough to go on. What's your excuse?

BLAIR. Professional. Took years to eradicate the twang —along with my past. (*a beat*) Sometimes I regret that.

GUS. Why?

BLAIR. Well, it's rather like the way I speak. I have what is known as a mid-Atlantic accent. The problem is that nobody *lives* in the mid-Atlantic.

GUS. I had you pegged as real Ivy League.

BLAIR. No, I had just enough education to know I was uneducated. So I read. For a while I embarrassed everybody, including myself, by actually quoting Goethe in Las Vegas lounges. Do you mind if I put on some music? It might help unjangle my nerves.

GUS. I'm leaving anyway. (*She moves to select tape as he puts on his jacket.*)

BLAIR. Even my name is not my own. My real name is Bernice. Bernice Gropes. (*makes a face*) Sounded like something I *did*. So I changed it. But sometimes when I look in the mirror I think of Gertrude Stein's line: "There's no there there." And there I go again. (*She inserts tape.*) By the way, *your* character is coming along nicely!

GUS. (*puzzled*) What character?

BLAIR. The colorful, self-deprecating, hard-drinking, disillusioned but still romantic maverick with the touch-of-a-poet character. (*He is just staring at her.*) When I met you in Boston it was almost there but it still needed work. But now you really *own* the part. The cigarette holder is new, isn't it? Nice idiosyncratic touch. (*His face gradually breaks into an amazed, admiring look and he shakes his head.*)

GUS. You are a real daisy, you know that? (*She smiles, turns away to start tape recorder.*)

BLAIR. Piercing masks is part of my profession. (*Mahler's Symphony #4 is heard on the stereo. It plays until indicated.*)

GUS. (*drily*) And what do you see, Doctor?

BLAIR. You're ambitious, devious, opportunistic, and there's a faint pervasive whiff of decadence about you.

GUS. No good qualities?

BLAIR. Those *are* the good qualities. (*They look at one another for a moment before he grins. She smiles back.*)

GUS. (*finally*) Well, I'd better get out of here and rehearse some more.

BLAIR. You look tired, Gus. Are you hungry? I could fix you some dinner.

GUS. I'm sure you want to be alone.

BLAIR. No. Not tonight. (*He looks at her.*)

GUS. You needn't be scared. I'm leaving four men at the entrance around the clock until we pick Lombardi up.

BLAIR. That's not why I asked you to stay. (*He looks at her, somewhat puzzled as he realizes her invitation is serious.*)

GUS. Yeah, well, I have some stuff to take care of in town.

BLAIR. (*gently*) Am I a suspect, Gus?

GUS. No, of course not. Why do you ask?

BLAIR. I thought your not staying might have something to do with — protocol. (*He is regarding her with a tinge of suspicion.*) You look puzzled. What is it?

GUS. (*finally*) I lost my fastball years ago, kid — I'm not sure I ever *had* one — but right now even my slow curve ball is barely getting over the plate.

BLAIR. I love it when you talk dirty. Now would you like to translate for the fans?

GUS. Why me?

BLAIR. Why not you?

GUS. I'm an overaged working stiff slightly on the re-pulsive side. (*She looks at him for a moment.*)

BLAIR. Either you don't know anything about women, which I doubt, or you've really been hurt badly by one, which I don't doubt at all.

GUS. So much for me. What about you?

BLAIR. (*simply; sincerely*) Right now, appearances to the contrary, I am not in wonderful shape and I could use some human — someone to — spiritually hold my hand. That's all. (*A small pause as he studies her; finally ca-pitulates.*)

GUS. I could come back in an hour or so. (*She beams a smile.*)

BLAIR. One more drink before you go? (*He shakes his head, reconsiders, nods. She moves to pour drink. He listens for a moment.*)

GUS. Is that the Von Karajan version? (*She turns.*) I have the Bernstein recording but I like this one almost as well. (*He moves* D.S., *absently patting his pockets.*)

BLAIR. That's very impressing.

GUS. That I listen to longhair music?

BLAIR. That you can tell the orchestra by the recording.

GUS. Oh, I used to be able to tell what *studio* the re-cording was made in. (*She turns back to bar.*)

BLAIR. Do you play an instrument? (*He is slowly moving across the stage, peering up, a frown on his face.*)

GUS. No, I just have a talent for appreciation and an acute ear for sounds — or combinations of sounds. (*He is now standing under a beam.*) Musical Idiot Savant. (*She turns from bar to find him gazing up at ceiling.*) It's a useless trick really — unless you happen to be a Doberman Pinscher attack dog.

BLAIR. What is it?

GUS. (*pointing*) I heard something from that beam.

BLAIR. They creak sometimes.

GUS. No, this wasn't creaking.

BLAIR. A scratching noise?

GUS. Yeah, sort of.

BLAIR. Oh, that's Millie.

GUS. Millie?

BLAIR. Millie the mouse. She's a field mouse who moves in about this time of year. Damned near killed me once.

GUS. How?

BLAIR. She dislodged one of those flower pots. Missed me by inches. That's why I put wicker ones up there. (*She moves to him with drink. Curiously:*) Did you always want to be a detective?

GUS. No, I wanted to be a voyeur. Being a cop just legalized it.

BLAIR. There are other professions that let you — look through other people's windows.

GUS. Sure. But I wasn't pretty enough to be a hooker, not patient enough to be a shrink, and my neck's too short for a clerical collar.

BLAIR. How about a writer?

GUS. Stiffs from my neighborhood didn't become

writers. Very few of them even became *readers*. (*He moves to deposit empty glass.*)

BLAIR. After "Scenario For Murder," I kept expecting another book.

GUS. (*drily*) So did I. Turned out I don't have the mind for complicated mystery plots.

BLAIR. Not like real life?

GUS. In police work I've found that the obvious usually turns out to be true. Also the hero or heroine gets killed at the end of Act One. (*There is a clap of thunder outside and rain starts to come down.*)

BLAIR. You sure you want to go out in that?

GUS. Have to. There may be some word on Lombardi. See you in about an hour and a half?

BLAIR. What time is it now?

GUS. (*checking watch*) Ten minutes to six.

BLAIR. My children should just be getting home from school in L.A. I have to talk to them before they have a chance to hear about — all this on the TV.

GUS. (*sympathetically*) Tough job.

BLAIR. Last unpleasant one of the day I hope. Afterwards I'm going to soak myself in some hot water for a very long time until I become a mindless prune. I mean if you're going to have wrinkles, have *wrinkles*. (*He nods, opens door.*) Oh, Gus. (*He turns.*) Thank you.

GUS. For what?

BLAIR. Being my friend. (*He nods and exits. BLAIR moves to stereo, turns off Mahler tape. She then moves to phone as GUS, unobserved by her, re-enters and watches as she dials first four numbers. The speaker is still on and we hear the dial tones. She notices him, stops dialing.*) What is it, Gus?

GUS. I forgot to ask — have you noticed if any valuables are missing? Furs, jewelry, that sort of thing.

BLAIR. I don't think so. Anyway, I don't own any furs and I never wear jewelry.

GUS. (*teasing*) No furs, no jewelry, no entourage. What kind of movie star are you anyway?

BLAIR. Faded. (*They look at one another for a moment.*)

GUS. Hey, are you okay?

BLAIR. I'm very resilient, Gus. I'll survive. (*He exits. BLAIR switches off speaker on phone, takes a deep breath as if preparing for the effort, re-dials number; into phone:*) Hello, may I speak to her please? — Blair Griffin — Yes, it is — I'm afraid so — I'm sorry you had to hear about it that way. I would have phoned you earlier but I was busy dealing with the police. Are the children home from school yet? — Oh. Well, when they get back would you keep them in the house and out of range of the TV or radio — No, I'd rather tell them about their father myself — I'm — I'm coping. The funeral is tomorrow and I'll be flying out the next morning. I'll be on *T.W.A.* Flight *42* and I'll be arriving at *1:45*. I'd appreciate if you'd meet me at the airport with them — Thanks.

(*She hangs up, rolls her head to relieve some tension, and then moves to turn out the lamps. The room is now illuminated by the burning fireplace logs and the light from the overhead skylight. She moves to stereo, selects a tape, exchanges it for the Mahler one still in cassette. She presses button and we hear Bartok's "Concerto for Orchestra." Quiet at first, faintly ominous. She then moves to door, bolts it. She then takes coffee things, moves into kitchen, deposits them, turns kitchen lights out, moves to jacuzzi controls, is about to push them when a wicker pot crashes down, just missing her. She jumps, looks*) *up at beam. She picks up potted plant, puts it on table. She then presses jacuzzi controls and crosses to couch, glancing up at beam as she goes. As she moves away, the jacuzzi top slides open. As she starts to undo robe, a soaking wet TONY LOMBARDI, holding the kitchen knife, leaps up out of the jacuzzi. BLAIR, her robe undone, turns, sees him standing with the knife in his hand. Both remain motionless for a long moment.*

Her *attitude, and the following action should be ambiguous. In other words, at this point, we should not know if she knew LOMBARDI was hiding in the jacuzzi all the time or whether she is desperately trying to control the situation. The music from the stereo rises to a loud, discordant pitch, and keeps pounding away through the following. BLAIR remains stock still as TONY, knife in hand, advances towards her. When he reaches her, he bends to put knife on coffee table, roughly embraces her. They sink to the floor, obscured from our view by the coffee table. We don't hear anything because of the music — but in the dim light we see the light, wicker sofa being jolted violently as the sex act takes place. Finally, it stops. A long moment before we see BLAIR's hand come above the coffee table and grasp the knife. We see the knife being held high, the blade picking up a shaft of light from above. It is plunged down with great force. After a moment, BLAIR scrambles to her feet and stares down, her eyes wide and trancelike. She shudders, pulls robe around her, blindly heads for the phone. She takes a deep breath, stands for a moment, controls her trembling hands and starts to dial. She stops as she hears something. TONY, the knife in his back, is pulling himself to his feet. He stands, weaving unsteadily, his eyes on BLAIR. He slowly staggers towards her, stops and we see his mouth form one word — "Why?" She hasn't moved. He continues towards her but sprawls to the floor at her feet. She stares down at him for a moment before she turns away and starts to dial as . . .)*

CURTAIN

End of Act One

ACT TWO

Scene 1

THE TIME: *An hour and a half later.*

AT RISE: *The stage is empty and dark except for the glowing embers in the fireplace and the fitful moonlight that shines through the windows and skylight. After a moment or two we hear footsteps outside the front door and see the bobbing beam of a flashlight. The front door is pushed open revealing the outline of a figure. The beam of the flashlight plays over the room before the figure moves to a lamp and turns it on. We now see that the figure is MAGGIE STRATTEN. She looks around the room which is exactly as we last saw it except that the jacuzzi top is closed. She studies the portrait of BLAIR for a moment, turns it so that it faces wall, shivers, puts the still lighted flashlight on the coffee table, moves to fireplace, picks up poker, hefts it, is about to poke embers but stops as she hears the sound of an approaching Jeep. Poker in hand, she quickly crosses to lamp, turns it off, looks out of window. Poker still in hand she moves to stairs, rapidly ascends them and exits into studio off landing as we hear the car motor turned off and the sound of approaching footsteps. The still lighted flashlight is sending out a slim beacon from the coffee table. At the last moment, MAGGIE reappears on the landing, races down the stairs, grabs the flashlight, and disappears into the studio again just as the front door is opened and the lights are turned on revealing GUS. He takes in room, moves to jacuzzi controls, finds button, and the jacuzzi top slides open. He moves to the open jacuzzi, sees something, kneels, pushes his sleeve up, puts his arm into water and pulls LOMBARDI's wet canvas bag out by the straps. He opens bag, takes out two cameras and some lenses that are all wrapped in waterproof plastic, MORGAN's wallet, watch and ring and the two silver candlesticks we saw earlier. He looks through wallet, puts it on the floor with the rest of the contents near the jacuzzi. He frowns, moves to stereo, rewinds tape, plays it, and we hear the Bartok "Concerto for Orchestra." He then moves to jacuzzi controls, moves away, his back to jacuzzi, takes off coat, turns, obviously reconstructing what has taken place. DORIS appears behind him in the doorway.*

DORIS. Musical appreciation hour? (*He turns, sees her, moves to turn off stereo.*) What is that?

GUS. Bartok.

DORIS. Noisy. (*He looks at her for a second.*)

GUS. Where's Blair?

DORIS. Waiting outside in the car. I thought I should make sure it was okay for her to come in.

GUS. How is she?

DORIS. Considering in one day she's watched her husband being stabbed to death and then was raped and killed another man — she's fair.

GUS. (*annoyed*) Will you give me a straight answer!

DORIS. (*simply*) The kid has a lot of guts. (*sees bag*) What's that?

GUS. Lombardi's bag. Husband's wallet, jewelry. (*DORIS moves over to look at it as GUS paces around.*)

DORIS. Anything useful in the wallet?

GUS. No. Lots of cash.

DORIS. (*looking around*) Doesn't look as if there was much of a struggle.

GUS. (*nettled*) She *told* us why. She thought if she stayed calm she could control the situation.

DORIS. Yeah, nerves of steel. Well, I'll tell you one thing that has come out of all this. Blair Griffin is big news again.

GUS. What the hell is that supposed to mean?

DORIS. Reporters are pouring into town.

GUS. So *what*?

DORIS. Why are you shouting?

GUS. I thought you said this house had been searched?

DORIS. How were we supposed to know there was a jacuzzi? The only person who knew about it was Blair and she didn't tell us. (*He is balefully surveying his appearance in mirror.*)

GUS. I didn't even know they'd *heard* of jacuzzi's in these parts. (*He starts to search his pockets for something.*)

DORIS. She had a crew fly in from Boston ten days ago and they put it in in one day. I checked. What are you looking for?

GUS. Do you have a comb?

DORIS. (*amazed*) You want to comb your hair?

GUS. (*irritably*) No, I want to stick it up my nose.

DORIS. I don't believe it.

GUS. Look, will you just give me the comb? (*She gets one from her bag, hands it to him during following.*)

DORIS. Didn't she tell you there was nothing missing?

GUS. Those candlesticks were easy to overlook. (*He glances over at jacuzzi, takes comb, combs hair through following.*) Do you think you could hear anything from under that top?

DORIS. Maybe footsteps, but that's about all. Those planks are two inches thick. Why?

GUS. Did the examination check out?

DORIS. Lombardi's semen was inside her, if that's what you mean. (*He looks at her for a moment, gives her back her comb.*)

GUS. Here.

DORIS. You look better.

GUS. Thanks.

DORIS. Now what are you going to do? Lose twenty pounds in the next three minutes?

GUS. Give me a break, will you, Doris. (*BLAIR appears at the door. She is wearing a rain slicker over the houserobe she is still wearing and looks pale and slightly disoriented.*) How are you?

BLAIR. Well, it hasn't been your average sort of day, has it? (*They look at one another for a moment.*)

GUS. Blair, do you have any idea how he knew about the jacuzzi?

BLAIR. He's been photographing this place for years. He knew every inch of the house.

GUS. When was the jacuzzi put in?

BLAIR. Just a few days ago—Oh, I see what you mean. Well, he'd been watching the place for the last day or so.

GUS. But how would he know how to open it?

BLAIR. I've been using it every day. I assume he must have been—(*She stops, shudders slightly.*) Nasty thought.

GUS. Where would he have been watching from?

BLAIR. What? Oh, there's a clear view of the switches from that big rock.

GUS. That's over a hundred yards away. (*She nods at photographic equipment by jacuzzi.*)

BLAIR. He had a telephoto lens, Gus. Look, would you

mind if I — get into something — more comfortable.

GUS. Of course not. (*She moves to stairs.*) Blair? (*She turns.*) I'm sorry.

BLAIR. My fault. (*She starts up stairs, stops.*) Oh, do me a favor. If there are any shots in there of me taking a jacuzzi, please don't sell them to the National Enquirer. My career's in enough trouble as it is without all those knees and nipples. (*GUS watches her as she exits to bedroom. DORIS looks up from where she has been kneeling by cameras.*)

DORIS. Gus, these cameras are wrapped in waterproof plastic.

GUS. I know that.

DORIS. That means that Lombardi could have known he was going to be in water *before* he left New York.

GUS. Or that he makes his living with his cameras and he protects them against moisture at all times. (*He drifts over to the phone.*)

DORIS. How did he get in the jacuzzi? (*GUS nods over at controls.*)

GUS. Try it. (*DORIS moves to controls, presses button, moves back to jacuzzi. We see that it closes slowly enough for someone to have time to climb in after pressing button.*)

DORIS. Okay. How did he think he was going to get out? (*GUS takes receiver off hook, presses speaker button, absently pushes dial buttons through following.*)

GUS. You just heard her. He knew she took one every day. Sooner or later she was going to open that top. Anyway, he didn't know that once inside he couldn't get out.

DORIS. How do you know?

GUS. He tried. There were wood splinters on the knife.

DORIS. Some other things bother me.

GUS. Oh, been playing detective have we?

DORIS. (*flaring*) Well, someone has to, because you're sure as hell not!

GUS. What?

DORIS. Oh, come off it, Gus—you've got a big thing about her!

GUS. (*moving away*) I'm too old to have "things." Especially big ones.

DORIS. Like hell! You're exactly the right age!

GUS. Have you been talking to my mother? I mean, how come you suddenly became such an expert on this particular menopausal maelstrom?

DORIS. Because she's your *type*!

GUS. (*thrown*) What?

DORIS. She even *looks* like Stephanie for God's sake! She's brighter, richer, more famous, more talented—the top of the line model. (*wryly*) Something you've always wanted. (*He looks at her for a moment.*)

GUS. You know, I liked you a lot better when I was your idol.

DORIS. So did I. (*a beat*) Look, could we talk about this in a professional manner for just a few moments? There are some things that keep running through my head.

GUS. Like what?

DORIS. Why did he make it look like a robbery?

GUS. Maybe he didn't make it look like a robbery. Maybe it *was* a robbery. (*He shrugs.*) He needed the dough, so he took the money and jewelry as an afterthought.

DORIS. Just so it wouldn't be a total loss?

GUS. Look, let me ask *you* some questions. Let's say —just for the sake of argument—that Blair was somehow involved in all this. Why would she want her husband dead?

DORIS. Jealousy?

GUS. She waits six months after she's discovered the affair? You really buy that?

DORIS. Revenge?

GUS. In that case, wouldn't she kill Maggie Stratten?

DORIS. Have you verified with Maggie that she and Morgan were having an affair?

GUS. (*nods*) That's who I was with when I got the call about the rape. I went right from there to the hospital.

DORIS. Lombardi?

GUS. Past help. Okay, let's skip over the rather crucial fact that we can't even *think* of a motive. How did she persuade Lombardi to kill Morgan?

DORIS. Money?

GUS. I see — she paid money to a man — totally inexperienced in killing — with no plan for him to escape. Anyway, if she knew he was in the jacuzzi why did she ask me to stay for dinner? (*She looks at him for a moment.*)

DORIS. Yeah — well, I'm glad we had this little talk, Inspector. (*She moves to gather up LOMBARDI's bag and contents.*)

GUS. Look, Doris, a theoretical case can be made against just about anybody if you let your imagination run rampant. Maggie Stratten? Maybe Morgan was planning on going back to Blair. Listen, I could make a case against me. Even you. (*She looks at him.*)

DORIS. That might be hard to do.

GUS. (*shrugs*) You were around when her first husband was killed and you — look, I'm no good at fiction. I'm just making a point. (*She nods.*) Hey, kid. Sorry I yelled at you.

DORIS. I think I was the one who yelled at you.

GUS. You're so competitive. (*She checks watch, moves to phone.*)

DORIS. I have to call L.A. and see what flight Joe's putting the kids on.

GUS. From here?

DORIS. I'll call collect.

(*As she dials 0-213-476-3412, we hear the dial tones on the speaker phone. GUS moves D.S., looks out, lights cigarette during following. We hear phone ringing through speaker, and then OPERATOR's VOICE.*)

OPERATOR'S VOICE. (*on speaker*) Operator.

DORIS. I'm placing a collect person-to-person call to a Joe Aylesworth in L.A. The number is 213-476-3412. My name is Doris Aylesworth and the number I'm calling from is 617-431-2240. (*We hear a recorded message.*)

JOE'S VOICE. (*on speaker*) If this is my agent, I know you said you'd call back, but that was a year ago. I waited but I have to go out now. Please leave your message at the sound of the beep.

OPERATOR'S VOICE. (*on speaker*) There's no answer at that number.

DORIS. Thanks, I'll call back. (*She switches phone off.*) Joe always was a million laughs. You coming in with me? (*GUS is still gazing out of window, musing.*) Gus?

GUS. What? Oh, no. I'll be in later. (*DORIS heads for door with bag.*) Oh, listen, will you give me a list of all outgoing calls from this place over the last ten days?

DORIS. Why?

GUS. Just do it, will you, Doris!

DORIS. You're yelling again.

(*BLAIR, wearing different clothes, appears on landing. She still appears rather disoriented.*)

BLAIR. Did someone call?

DORIS. No. I was trying to call my ex-husband in L.A. Collect. That all? (*GUS nods.*) Goodnight, Miss Griffin.

BLAIR. Goodnight, Doris. (*GUS opens door for DORIS and she exits. He closes door behind her.*) How long has she been in love with you? (*He turns to look at her.*)

GUS. Doris? I've known her since she was a kid. Her old man used to own the bike shop here.

BLAIR. Even so — she worships you.

GUS. Oh, *worships* — that's another thing. I helped her get into the police academy.

BLAIR. Oh, well, that explains everything. (*He looks at her for a moment.*)

GUS. (*awkwardly*) This is a fairly isolated place, Blair. It's more — an affair of convenience than passion.

BLAIR. I think you settle too easily.

GUS. Maybe you're right. (*They hold the contact for a moment.*) How you feeling?

BLAIR. Numb. As if I'm — sleepwalking. My mind is — not functioning efficiently. (*She moves away.*)

GUS. (*gently*) Blair, why don't you sit down?

BLAIR. No, I'm all right. (*She moves to bar, takes glass and bottle and prepares to pour drink.*) You know, it's strange how even after — something like tonight — the body reasserts itself. I'm hungry. Rather comforting. A nice, normal — (*The glass shatters in her hand. She looks at her fingers, speaks in an oddly calm voice.*) Oh, dear, now I've cut myself. It's strange. The sight of blood has always fascinated me. When I was a little girl I had a microscope — (*She turns to face him — quietly, tightly.*) I hate this. I really do. (*He quickly moves to her.*)

GUS. It's okay, Blair. Let go — just let go. (*She stares at him with vulnerable, wide, dry eyes.*)

BLAIR. I — I don't know how, Gus.

GUS. Okay, don't talk. Let me see. (*He examines her finger.*)

BLAIR. My God, what a *girlish* thing to do.

GUS. Let me put something on it. You have a first aid kit?

BLAIR. Over there. (*He moves to first aid kit.*)

GUS. Sit down and hold your finger up. (*She sits, watches him as he opens first aid kit.*)

BLAIR. Have you ever killed anyone, Gus? (*He turns to look at her.*)

GUS. Yes.

BLAIR. Do you still think about it?

GUS. You didn't mean to kill him.

BLAIR. Oh, yes I did. (*He regards her for a moment, turns away.*)

GUS. You had no other choice, Blair.

BLAIR. I don't *know* that. (*He looks at her.*) It's probably true, but I don't know and never will. How did you deal with that? (*He moves to her with kit.*)

GUS. You learn to live with it. Hold still for a moment. This may hurt for a second. (*She doesn't flinch as he applies antiseptic.*)

BLAIR. Who is Stephanie? (*He looks at her, thrown.*)

GUS. What?

BLAIR. I suppose I should have warned you that from my bathroom one can hear everything that's said in this room. (*He looks at her, his mind clicking back over the conversation between he and DORIS. He starts to put band aid on.*) Who's Stephanie?

GUS. Be careful. You're liable to get the whole sorry, sentimental saga.

BLAIR. Those are the sagas I like the best. (*He looks

at her.) Make a fire and tell me a bedtime story, Gus. I need the distraction. (*He looks at her for a moment, moves to get kindling and logs.*)

GUS. I was married — two kids. I didn't really realize how much trouble our marriage was in until our twentieth anniversary — and I had the nasty little thought that if I'd killed her on our honeymoon I'd have been out for five years now. (*He starts to put wood in grate.*) Anyway, I was working in the narcotic division out of Boston and was assigned the porno movie ring case and — well, I got lucky.

BLAIR. I read your book, Gus. It wasn't luck.

GUS. I know — I was being modest. (*He puts match to wood.*) When the book took off, a couple of national magazines did profiles that made me seem like a combination of Sam Spade and Albert Schweitzer. I was hotter than this year's blonde and more popular than the flavor of the month. I reacted like any normal, red-blooded, American middle-aged sap. I became — impossible.

BLAIR. You liked being famous?

GUS. I was both attracted and repelled by it. (*a beat*) And even some of the things that repelled me I found attractive.

BLAIR. I know what you mean.

GUS. Anyway, I met a girl. Hell, I met a lot of girls. (*He glances at her.*) I know this may be hard to believe but, before this, I was never what you'd call a fast worker.

BLAIR. Not even when you were single?

GUS. Never went to bed with a girl I hadn't had Thanksgiving dinner with. Anyway, I met a girl. She was a former Miss Massachusetts, now a local TV weather person. Perfect, right?

BLAIR. Stephanie.

GUS. The very same. So there she was — a twenty-two-year-old tootsie entirely to my liking. I should have known better—the danger signals were in neon. I mean apart from her tender years she was my type.

BLAIR. You think men have types?

GUS. (*drily*) Well, at my age, it's more a question of gender. Naturally I fell in love and then—just to finish the disaster—I left my wife, moved in with Stephanie, quit the force, and settled down to make a public spectacle of myself. (*He absently looks around for poker.*)

BLAIR. I think you're being too hard on yourself. (*He stops looking for poker, nudges log with his foot.*)

GUS. No, life didn't need any help from me on that score. (*He sits, thinks for a moment.*) My son, David— he was seventeen at the time—was having trouble with his mother. She was drinking and—well, the upshot was, I asked him to move in with us. I finally started writing a new book—fiction—and everything seemed to be hunky-dory. A regular Hallmark card. Dave and Stephanie were getting along great—well, why wouldn't they? They were the same generation. Can you guess the rest?

BLAIR. It *is* classic. (*a beat*) Are they still together?

GUS. As far as I know. (*in response to her look*) I suppose that's the worst part of it. I lost my son, too. (*He gets up, moves away to look out of window.*)

BLAIR. You can't forgive him?

GUS. Sure—*now* I could. The kid's too embarrassed to talk to me.

BLAIR. Is that why you said you could understand someone killing out of jealousy? (*He turns to look at her, gives a small shrug.*) What did you do?

GUS. Well, I'd already gone through the advance for my nonexistent second book. So there I was, a dispirited Lancelot, nursing my deeply wounded aspirations and facing an impenitent, old age. I confronted the bitter, unpalatable truth, called in a couple of favors and managed to get myself assigned here to oblivion where I've been working on the role of the town character. How am I doing?

BLAIR. I think you're miscast. Too much life left in you yet. (*They look at each other for a moment.*)

GUS. You still want that drink?

BLAIR. Scotch, please. Maybe it'll help me sleep. (*He moves to pour drinks through following.*)

GUS. The doctor didn't give you any tranquilizers?

BLAIR. No. It's the one time I could have used one, but he didn't think to offer and I didn't think to ask.

GUS. Would you like me to get you some?

BLAIR. Bit late.

GUS. It's no problem. I used to be a narc, remember. I have a bathroom closet that looks like Walgreens.

BLAIR. You use pills?

GUS. Are you kidding? I take a valium to put my contact lenses in. I could send some out.

BLAIR. It's not necessary, Gus. Believe it or not, I'm beginning to relax. I suppose at one point, the nervous system says, "All right, enough craziness, everybody. We all have to go to sleep now." (*He hands her drink.*)

GUS. (*toasts*) To friendship.

BLAIR. That's a very good toast. (*He is staring at her.*) What is it?

GUS. I'm going to miss you.

BLAIR. I'll be back. Men like you are hard to come by.

GUS. (*finally*) Dime a dozen, kid.

BLAIR. No, you're very special. (*He hasn't taken his eyes from her.*) I knew it when we met four years ago. We talked for less than an hour, but something happened between us, didn't it, Gus? Something really — nice.

Gus. Nice. That's rather like saying "For a fat guy he doesn't sweat much." (*She smiles.*)

Blair. Oh, I'm not saying I heard a full philharmonic orchestra. But over the years you would pop into my head at unexpected moments. All very odd. Have I embarrassed you?

Gus. Yes—but it's a nice feeling.

Blair. Well, at my age coyness is unbecoming. Anyway, I thought your knowing might be good for you.

Gus. You mean for my ego.

Blair. No. For your soul. (*They are gazing at each other when the phone rings. BLAIR moves to pick it up.*) Hello—Oh, hello, Doris—Yes, he's right here. (*She holds phone out for GUS.*) Doris. I think she's checking up on us. (*as he takes phone*) I'm going to get something to eat. (*BLAIR exits to kitchen as GUS talks into phone.*)

Gus. (*into phone*) What's up?—oh, right—well, are there many, because I can wait and look at the list when —Oh, okay, go ahead—uh-huh—uh-huh—uh-huh— uh-huh. (*His expression changes.*) Wait a minute, are you sure about that?—The last call at five-fifty this afternoon. Give me that again—Hold on. (*He looks around, finds telephone book near phone, checks area code numbers at front of book.*) Yeah, I'm still here—No, nothing. Thanks, Doris. (*He hangs up, a puzzled expression on his face. BLAIR enters from kitchen eating a banana.*)

Blair. Best natural food in the world. Easy to digest, loaded with potassium and—(*She stops as she sees his expression.*) Is something the matter?

Gus. No. Why?

Blair. You're looking a little like a puzzled Basset hound who doesn't quite know what to make of the scent.

GUS. Chronic expression if you're a cop. Goes with the flat feet. It's a kit.

BLAIR. (*holding up banana*) You want one of these?

GUS. No, thanks. I have to get some paperwork done. (*He moves to get his coat.*) You going to be okay?

BLAIR. Now I am. (*a beat as they look at each other*) Will I see you at the funeral tomorrow?

GUS. I'm sorry, kid. I'd like to be there but I don't think I'll be back in time.

BLAIR. Back from where?

GUS. I have to go to Washington.

BLAIR. I wish you didn't.

GUS. It's my daughter. She's a music major at Georgetown and is giving her first solo recital tomorrow.

BLAIR. Then you definitely have to go. What is she playing?

GUS. (*doesn't skip a beat*) The Korngold concerto.

BLAIR. She must be a very good pianist.

GUS. Violinist. It's a concerto for violin, Blair.

BLAIR. Of course. Will I be allowed to leave the day after tomorrow?

GUS. I don't see why not. Anxious to get back to your kids?

BLAIR. (*nods*) There's a flight out of Boston for L.A. early in the morning. (*He nods.*) I *will* see you before I leave?

GUS. I'll meet you here after the funeral. (*She moves to him, kisses him in a manner more affectionate than passionate, but with overtones of something in the air. They break.*) Sleep tight, kid.

(*He exits. She watches him go, a reflective look on her face, and then crosses to the stereo. She takes out tape, looks at it, shudders slightly, throws it in waste-*

basket. She then looks for another tape, finds it, inserts it and we hear the Korngold "Concerto for Violin." She moves across the room, stops in front of one of the dolls, picks it up, holds it up in front of her and then slowly waltzes around the room with it, gradually whirling faster and faster. She stops in front of the fire, hugs the doll to her chest, and stares reflectively into the fire, the flames illuminating her face in the dimly lit room.

MAGGIE STRATTEN, poker in hand, silently appears on the landing and stands for a moment observing BLAIR who is unaware of her presence. MAGGIE quietly comes down stairs, moves to a few feet behind BLAIR.)

MAGGIE. How you doing, babe? (*BLAIR turns.*)

BLAIR. (*finally*) Why are you here, Maggie?

MAGGIE. I bought a flashlight and walked out. I thought you'd be alone by the time I got here.

BLAIR. He could have spotted you.

MAGGIE. If he had, I'd have told him that you were going to give me some of Morgan's paintings.

BLAIR. (*firmly*) This is *my* script, Maggie. Don't ad lib — it's sloppy and very dangerous!

MAGGIE. (*simply*) I had to see you. (*BLAIR nods, moves to her, and the two women embrace. They break.*) You were wonderful.

BLAIR. So were you.

MAGGIE. I always was, when I had good material. (*BLAIR moves to stereo, clicks it off as MAGGIE moves to deposit poker by fireplace.*) Pretty.

BLAIR. Korngold Concerto. (*The two women look at one another a moment before BLAIR impulsively moves back to her, embraces and kisses her passionately. They break and MAGGIE regards BLAIR's feverish expression.)*

MAGGIE. You're completely unpredictable.

BLAIR. Not really. Danger always — gets my juices going. (*She touches MAGGIE's face.*) You feel cold, Maggie.

MAGGIE. Yes, well fear has that effect on *me*. (*She sits on sofa.*)

BLAIR. I told you there was no reason to be afraid. (*She stretches out, puts her head in MAGGIE's lap. MAGGIE strokes her hair.*) It was almost too easy.

MAGGIE. I'm still worried, babe. The man's not dumb.

BLAIR. I know. Wouldn't have been as much fun if he was. (*MAGGIE stops stroking her hair.*)

MAGGIE. Fun? You really think it was fun? (*BLAIR looks at her, changes her attitude.*)

BLAIR. Of course not. It was — something that had to be done. It had to be done, Maggie. (*She sighs.*) Anyway, it's all over.

MAGGIE. Don't take any bows yet. I phoned my office in L.A. Somebody has been sniffing around asking questions.

BLAIR. (*unconcerned*) Probably Doris. She's jealous of me. Doesn't mean a thing.

MAGGIE. I wish I had your supreme confidence.

BLAIR. Maggie, he's bought everything.

MAGGIE. Supposing he hasn't? (*BLAIR looks at her for a second, shrugs, and speaks in a casual tone that makes what she says all the more chilling.*)

BLAIR. Oh, then we'll just have to kill him. (*MAGGIE is staring at her. BLAIR smiles and . . .*)

CURTAIN

End of Act Two, Scene 1

Scene 2

The Time: *Late afternoon, the next day.*

At Rise: *The lamps have not been turned on but we can discern GUS sitting alone on the stage, smoking, an open bottle of Scotch beside him. He looks better-groomed than before and is wearing a sports coat, shirt, tie, etc. The Korngold "Concerto for Violin" is playing on the stereo. He takes a gulp of Scotch, stubs out his cigarette with a frustrated, angry gesture, rises and starts to pace. He stops as he notices one of the dolls. He picks it up, studies it for a moment, shakes his head, and suddenly, angrily hurls it across the room. The front door opens and we see the outline of BLAIR standing in the doorway. She flicks a light switch and the room becomes illuminated revealing that she is wearing a dark suit appropriate for a funeral, a hat, and a small veil. The two look at one another for a moment before he moves to turn off the stereo.*

Blair. I'm glad you're here. (*She moves to him and embraces him.*) When did you get back?

Gus. About four drinks ago.

Blair. You came right from the airport? (*He nods.*)

Gus. How did the funeral go?

Blair. All right. The best thing about it is that it's over. (*She moves away, removes hat and veil and tosses them aside.*) The press were reasonably well behaved. At least nobody stuck a microphone in my face during the service. Maggie made rather a fool of herself which raised a few eyebrows, but I suppose we should feel thankful she didn't actually throw herself on the grave. (*He has been watching her with enigmatic eyes.*) You look different.

Gus. I shaved.

BLAIR. No, it's something else.

GUS. I saw your children, Blair. (*a pause*)

BLAIR. How are they?

GUS. Very healthy.

BLAIR. (*finally*) You're a very good liar. I believed you really did have a daughter in college in Washington.

GUS. No. She's a computer programmer in Cincinnati.

BLAIR. I do believe I need a drink. (*She moves to bar to pour herself one.*) Should I call my lawyer, Gus?

GUS. I don't have enough to arrest you yet.

BLAIR. What do you have?

GUS. Enough facts to build a probable scenario. (*BLAIR is looking at herself in the mirror.*)

BLAIR. Probable?

GUS. There are still a couple of holes, but it's almost finished.

BLAIR. I look ridiculous. I feel like a female impersonator doing Joan Crawford. (*She turns to look at him.*) Don't look so sad, Gus. Maybe I can help you fill in the holes. (*She moves to lightly touch his cheek.*) Come on, don't look at me like that. Everything will be all right. I promise. (*She moves away.*) Why don't you tell me about your scenario?

GUS. Not mine. Yours.

BLAIR. Let's not fight over credits. (*She takes off shoes, throws them aside.*) You know, I thought I was doing so well. What started you digging?

GUS. Bartok. I wondered why anyone would play Bartok's "Concerto for Orchestra" when they wanted to relax in a jacuzzi. (*He moves to pour himself another drink.*)

BLAIR. My taste in music led you to Washington?

GUS. No. That was something that happened the day before. You said your children were in L.A., but something kept nagging at me about the way you made that call. I've called L.A. enough times, but I didn't pin down what didn't sit right until later. (*He moves to phone, flicks on speaker phone, pushes 1-213. We hear the dial tones.*) That's L.A. (*He disconnects, pushes 1-202. We hear the dial tones.*) That's Washington.

BLAIR. You *do* have a good ear.

GUS. Not that good. But when Doris called L.A. something clicked in my head and I decided to run a check of telephone calls from this house during the past ten days. The call you made at 5:50 wasn't to L.A., it was to Washington. I couldn't fathom why you would lie or why you'd be calling the Dean of some private prep school for girls. When I found out her Ph.D. was in Art History I thought the connection was worth a trip.

BLAIR. You saw the good doctor?

GUS. (*nods*) That's when I met your children.

BLAIR. What did she tell you?

GUS. That she and Morgan were to be married in a week. (*She looks at him for a moment.*)

BLAIR. I'm surprised she even agreed to talk to you.

GUS. I promised to keep her name out of the papers if it was at all possible.

BLAIR. Yes, Ruth is very respectable, isn't she? (*She moves to get her drink.*)

GUS. She's in a very bad way. (*She turns to look at him.*) Of course, she didn't suspect you had anything to do with Morgan's death. She just kept repeating how senseless it all was.

BLAIR. (*steadily*) Sometimes people get hurt by flying debris, Gus. (*She puts her drink down.*)

GUS. She told me that you had agreed to let her and Morgan have custody of your children. (*BLAIR looks at him for a moment, nods, and then starts to take off her blouse. It should not appear to be deliberately provocative but rather casual. He is staring at her.*) What are you doing?

BLAIR. I have to get out of these clothes.

GUS. I can wait while you change.

BLAIR. No, I'm really interested in what you have to say. (*He stares at her as she starts to get out of her skirt, pulls his eyes away, moves to window.*)

GUS. I believe you adore your children, Blair. I couldn't imagine that anyone in the world could make you voluntarily give them up. (*He turns from the window. She is standing in a black slip watching him. He regards her for a moment, starts moving again.*) So much for facts. The rest is a scenario. (*She sits with drink.*)

BLAIR. I didn't think you were any good at fiction.

GUS. No, but if you have a solid premise, sometimes the rest will almost write itself.

BLAIR. What's the premise, Gus?

GUS. It's based on the big lie. If the big lie worked — everything worked.

BLAIR. And what's the big lie?

GUS. Maggie Stratten. She wasn't having an affair with your husband. She was the decoy — the decoy to stop me looking for the real other woman — Ruth. Because Ruth could provide the critical missing element — a motive for you to have your husband killed. (*She smiles.*) Why the hell are you smiling?

BLAIR. I'm always pleased when my instincts prove correct. (*She moves to him, lightly touches him.*) I just knew you were bright. (*He doesn't respond, but we can see he is disconcerted by her attitude and closeness.*) Go on.

GUS. I started asking myself some questions. (*She*

nods, moves away.) First question: what made you agree to give Morgan and Ruth custody of your children? Natural conclusion—blackmail. (*She turns to look at him.*) But what could he possibly be blackmailing you with? What could you have done that if known would be so hurtful you'd agree to anything? I came up blank. (*She doesn't help him.*) Next question: why did Maggie Stratten agree to collaborate with you—play out that whole charade for me so that you would then confide that she was your husband's lover?

BLAIR. She was very good, wasn't she? (*She moves to look out of window.*) Of course she used to be an actress.

GUS. But why would she implicate herself in a murder? (*She turns to look at him.*)

BLAIR. Murder? (*He nods.*) So you think I got Lombardi to kill Morgan?

GUS. Yeah, I'm afraid I do.

BLAIR. How did I do that, Gus?

GUS. (*finally*) I don't know. That's the hole. I just don't know.

BLAIR. Very big hole, don't you think? Especially in a courtroom. (*He breaks eye contact with her, moves away.*)

GUS. I do have an idea of why Lombardi made it look like a break-in and robbery though. Two months ago when you took him to court—and that's *why* you took him to court, so you could make contact with him and outline your plan—you told him you'd tell the police it was an unknown intruder. You'd make up a description and the police would go off on a wild goose chase. Later, you and he could leave the island unsuspected. (*She regards him for a moment.*)

BLAIR. Are you hungry? I'm absolutely starved. (*He*

stares at her.) I put some fruit and cheese out before I left for the funeral. (*moving towards kitchen*) I suspected you might want something after your flight.

Gus. (*incredulously angry*) Are you going to serve goddamned coffee again!

Blair. I can listen from the kitchen, Gus. You go ahead. (*She exits to kitchen. He stands, his emotions churning.*)

Blair. (*offstage*) Go on—I can hear you perfectly.

Gus. You didn't keep your word with Lombardi. You had your own scheme and you'd planned everything months ago.

Blair. (*offstage*) Everything?

Gus. (*angrily*) Everything—the jacuzzi, the rape, the killing—everything.

(*BLAIR enters carrying the same cheeseboard we saw in Scene 1. It contains fruit, cheese, bread—and a long kitchen knife. GUS spots the knife immediately but tries not to show it. She has stopped and the two are looking at one another.*)

Blair. Have you told anyone else any of this?

Gus. No.

Blair. Why not? (*a small pause*)

Gus. I just didn't. (*He watches her as she moves to table, puts cheeseboard down.*) Tell me it's not true, Blair. (*She turns to look at him.*)

Blair. I can't. It's all true. (*She turns back to cheeseboard, takes knife out of cheese.*) Would you like me to tell you what happened? (*She cuts a slice from an apple.*) I think it's about time I produced a character witness, don't you? (*She moves away, taking the apple and the knife with her.*) All my life, people have left me. My father, my first husband—oh, he didn't physically leave me, but he was drinking so much he was mentally gone —the men I knew between marriages—they all left me, did you know that? (*He shakes his head.*) It seems my— appeal tends to fade—over the long haul. (*She gives a little shrug.*) Then I married Morgan and the two children were born. (*She cuts another slice of apple.*) Do you know the greatest thing about having them? I finally had two people who would never leave me. I was their mother and nobody could ever take them away. Ever. (*She makes an unformed gesture.*) I was shooting a film in Washington. That's when Morgan met Ruth. She was a great admirer of his work, heard he was in town and invited him out to her school to lecture. When I found out, Maggie flew in to—hold my hand. (*She moves to him, slowly raises knife with slice of apple on it to his chest level.*) You want some apple? (*He shakes head. She takes apple, moves away with knife.*) About Maggie. She makes careers—she's that powerful. When she approached me to become a client, I was flattered—but puzzled. I simply wasn't in the same class as the rest of her clients. But my career desperately needed help, so I didn't ask any questions. Of course, now I know she signed me because she had a—thing about me. (*There is a pause.*)

GUS. (*finally*) She's queer?

BLAIR. You mean gay?

GUS. No, I mean queer.

BLAIR. Oh, I forgot—you don't like to add words.

GUS. I don't like to lose them either. Is she?

BLAIR. Yes. (*a slight shrug*) If you kept digging you'd have found out sooner or later. (*He shakily takes out a cigarette, starts to pat his pockets for a match.*) You need a light? (*He regards her for a second.*)

GUS. No, I was looking for something to wipe the egg off my face. (*He moves to pour himself a healthy slug of Scotch with a trembling hand.*)

BLAIR. The information doesn't warrant that big a drink, Gus.

GUS. Oh, that was the *good* news? (*She moves back to table, sticks the knife in the cheese, turns to him, shrugs.*)

BLAIR. Look, I tend to attract gays, but I could always handle it and — since we're being very honest — sometimes I've even used it. (*She starts to move away from table, leaving knife in cheese. He notices this.*) But Maggie is something else. Don't be fooled by that warm, funny mask she wears. She's — (*She stops, moves back to table, picks up knife.*) She's one tough, shrewd operator. (*She moves away, taking knife with her.*) Anyway, when I found out about Morgan, I was — devastated. Maggie flew in, I was vulnerable and — well — (*She looks at him.*) Look, normally it would all have been over in two weeks — a fiction that didn't work anymore — but I was in such a state of emotional disarray that I was fairly open about our attachment. Morgan learned about it and I didn't even bother to deny it. I suppose in some way it was a method of — striking back. (*She pauses, studies knife blade for a moment.*) Is it beginning to all come together?

GUS. He threatened to make it public if you didn't give him the children.

BLAIR. Yes.

GUS. The courts don't automatically give the husband child custody just because of lesbian affairs.

BLAIR. No, but it would have been very — messy. The important thing is that it would have changed my children's image of me.

GUS. If they could read.

BLAIR. (*intensely*) What about the future? (*She shakes*

head.) It was the most vicious, cruel thing I'd ever encountered. (*She looks at him.*) He knew I loved them, he knew that nobody could be a better parent. (*quietly intense*) And I'd rather die than lose them. I mean that literally. I could say that everything I did was to protect them, but that would only be partially true. (*a beat*) The real truth is that, without them, I couldn't survive, because—without them, I am nothing. (*She is trembling slightly. She regains control.*) Sorry to get so intense. Kids'll do it to me every time. (*She moves to window, looks out.*)

GUS. And of course there was your career. (*She looks at him.*) Oh, it wouldn't have ruined every career, but yours is based on—a certain sex image—and it would have stopped it dead in its tracks.

BLAIR. (*mildly*) We all have to make a living, Gus.

GUS. Yes, we do.

BLAIR. Would you like to know how I got Lombardi to kill Morgan? (*He doesn't say anything.*) It's funny. Do you remember when you were discussing motives for murder you mentioned blackmail? (*He nods.*) Right area, wrong direction. (*He doesn't understand.*) It's like one of those many-sided glass gismos—the ones that you hold up to the light. (*She raises knife up so the light catches the blade.*)

GUS. A prism.

BLAIR. Yes. Well, imagine yourself holding it up. You have a certain picture. But now turn it slightly—(*She changes slant of blade.*) Now you get a different slant, don't you? (*She lowers knife, looks at him.*) Gus, he'd been watching me for fifteen years. Always on the outside looking in. Now turn it around.

GUS. You were on the inside looking out watching him.

BLAIR. Right. We both knew enough to hang each other.

GUS. Literally?

BLAIR. He killed my first husband.

GUS. (*finally*) Lombardi murdered him?

BLAIR. Not exactly. But he contributed to his death — probably caused it. Jerry was drunk, we got into a fight, he beat the hell out of me and left. It was pouring with rain and he was in no condition to drive, but there was no way to stop him — I'm not sure I even wanted to. I stood right here and watched him drive off. The car was veering from side to side, but he'd driven this road, drunk and sober, many times before. As the car reached Randall's Point, Lombardi stepped out from behind — (*She points.*) — that tree and took a flash photo at practically point blank range. The flash must have blinded Jerry, the car swerved, went through the guardrail and over the cliff into the ocean.

GUS. And if you ever told the police what had happened, Lombardi would be prosecuted.

BLAIR. That was the implication. Of course, the fact that he was obsessed with me helped, too. The threat was really just something to tip him over the edge. (*GUS looks at her with incredulity. She smiles back.*)

GUS. You're incredible.

BLAIR. In what way?

GUS. The way you've gathered all your cards over the years — selecting, discarding, until you had an unbeatable hand.

BLAIR. Not unbeatable. There was always the wild card of Ruth. Of course the gamble wasn't whether you'd find her but whether she'd find you.

GUS. What made you bet on her not coming forward?

BLAIR. Because of the sort of person she is and because she had absolutely no reason to suspect any in-
volvement on my part.

GUS. She didn't know about Maggie or that Morgan
had used that information to get custody?

BLAIR. No, that was part of the agreement I made with
Morgan. Of course I couldn't be absolutely certain that
she wouldn't contact the police but one has to play the
percentages. Anyway, a small scent of danger always
adds to the game, don't you think?

GUS. (*finally*) Why'd you spill all the beans to me,
kid?

BLAIR. Because I have the knife. (*He looks at it. She
grins and sticks the knife in coffee table in front of sofa.*)
And I trust you.

GUS. I'm a cop. I could be wired.

BLAIR. You're not. I could tell when we embraced.

GUS. (*drily*) Nice to know you trust me.

BLAIR. Anyway, you can't prove a thing, can you?
(*She moves away.*) I mean, even if you wanted to.

GUS. There's still a faint residue of professional pride
floating around in me somewhere, kid.

BLAIR. I know. But there's one card I've been holding
back. A nice, warm, ace in the hole that if all else failed,
I could play.

GUS. What's that?

BLAIR. That you'd fall in love with me. (*He stares at
her, shakes his head, moves away from her, turns back.*)

GUS. You actually *planned* that?

BLAIR. No. But I saw — the possibility.

GUS. When?

BLAIR. When I saw Stephanie. (*He is staring at her.*)
She was the weather girl on that TV show we did.

GUS. That was four years ago.

BLAIR. It was just something I filed away. I had no plans then. That came later.

GUS. (*finally*) I'm beginning to seriously suspect — I am overmatched.

BLAIR. No, we're a perfect match. That's the whole point.

GUS. How — how could you be that sure?

BLAIR. Because I'm in love with you. And we're very much alike.

GUS. You think so?

BLAIR. We're two of a kind, Gus. We live by instinct, not convention. We've both been abandoned in various ways — and we both have our eye on the main chance. (*She shrugs.*) Our styles differ, that's all. (*quietly persuasive*) Come on, Gus. What do you have to look forward to here? Twenty more dreary years of prefabricated lays with Doris? (*She moves to him, intensely.*) We could have a *wonderful* life together. We'd have the best of everything — the best people, the best tables, the best seat in the grandstand, Gus. And when we got tired of the outside world, we'd have a *family.* My children would adore you. (*a beat*) Most of all, we'd have each other. (*He looks at her for a moment, abruptly moves away.*)

GUS. It's not possible, kid.

BLAIR. Yes, it is. There's only one stumbling block.

GUS. (*his back to her*) Maggie Stratten.

BLAIR. Yes, but that's no problem. (*He turns to look at her.*)

GUS. She'd give you up?

BLAIR. Of course not. She's not like that — she's a killer. (*She smiles.*) I think I warned you my sense of humor is a trifle macabre. No, we'll have to — take care of the problem ourselves.

GUS. (*finally*) How would we do that?

BLAIR. Simply. No frills, no risk.

GUS. Three deaths in four days? *Charles Dickens* would have trouble selling that.

BLAIR. He didn't live in America. All I need is a drug — a pill that will knock her out for ten — fifteen minutes. Is it possible for you to obtain that?

GUS. (*carefully*) It's possible.

BLAIR. Something that has no taste and, just to be on the safe side, leaves no trace. Something that could be put in — a glass of red wine. She drinks red wine.

GUS. Then what?

BLAIR. She passes out. I open the jacuzzi, put her in, close the top over her. I turn on the water — (*She moves to tap.*) — here. The jacuzzi fills up. She drowns. She'll be unconscious, Gus — completely painless. I then put her in her car — she doesn't weigh much, I can manage that — drive it two hundred yards to Randall's Point and let it roll over the edge into the sea. (*a beat*) An accident. Victim was drinking and didn't know the road — it's all happened before. Who knows? Something good could come out of this whole incident. Maybe they'll finally do something about that road. (*He doesn't smile. After a second he moves to look at tap for jacuzzi, looks at jacuzzi, then crosses to look out of window at Randall's Point.*) You don't even have to be here. All you have to do is provide the drug.

GUS. That's all?

BLAIR. No, there's one more thing. I'd really like you to make love to me. (*a beat*) And that's my final offer. (*He looks at her for a long moment, then moves to her in front of sofa. They gaze at one another for a moment before he bends down, takes knife from coffee table, moves away, puts knife in cheese, stands facing front*

for a moment, turns, moves back to BLAIR, kisses her,
and they start to make love as . . .)

CURTAIN

End of Act Two, Scene 2

SCENE 3

THE TIME: *Nine p.m. the next evening.*

AT RISE: *It is raining outside. A small table by the curtained window has been set for two. There is a bottle of red wine and two wine glasses but only one is full. The jacuzzi top is open and a hose snakes out of the tank and across the floor to the French windows. BLAIR is mopping up some water from the floor. The door opens and GUS, wearing a wet raincoat, enters and stops. She puts mop aside and moves to embrace him. They break.*

BLAIR. You're soaked. (*taking off his coat*) Here, let me get you out of this. (*He has noticed hose.*)

GUS. What's that? (*She moves away with his coat. We see he is wearing a gun and holster.*)

BLAIR. It drains the excess water out of the jacuzzi. (*She moves back to get mop.*)

GUS. Blair? (*She turns.*) Where's Maggie?

BLAIR. It's all over, Gus. (*GUS looks as if he's been poleaxed.*)

GUS. All over?

BLAIR. I was just mopping the floor. I didn't want the water to stain the wood.

GUS. (*unbelievingly*) She's dead. (*She looks at him for a moment.*)

BLAIR. Why do you seem so surprised?

GUS. (*carefully*) Everything went — according to plan? (*BLAIR mops up floor during following.*)

BLAIR. No, there was a slight hitch. (*He waits.*) Her car wouldn't start. I was worried that it might be the generator or the spark plugs but it was just a wet battery. Fortunately, I have a jump cable in my car and I used it. (*She moves to put mop away.*)

GUS. Where is the car now?

BLAIR. At the bottom of the cliff. It turned over on the way down so you can see the wheels sticking out of the water. (*He moves to look out of window.*) Can you see it?

GUS. No, it's too dark. The — the pills worked? (*She turns to look at him.*)

BLAIR. Oh, I didn't have to use them. (*He slowly sits.*) Actually, I couldn't get her to drink any wine. She barely touched it and then went right for the brandy. While I was wondering if the pills would be as effective in the brandy the question became academic.

GUS. (*his lips dry*) Why?

BLAIR. After five brandies she decided she wanted to take a jacuzzi. Ironic, right? I know from past experience that after seven drinks Maggie usually passes out. (*a slight shrug*) It made everything ridiculously simple. (*He doesn't say anything.*) We're home free, Gus. It's all over. (*He slowly stands, shakes head.*) What is it?

GUS. You can't be that casual. You just can't be. (*She looks at him for a long moment.*)

BLAIR. (*finally — her voice cracking slightly*) I told you I was a bad actress. (*a beat*) Would you please hold me, Gus? Right now I need — someone to hold onto. (*She moves to him and clings to him very tightly for a long moment. They break.*) First time I've seen you with a gun. You look like a cop.

Gus. Sometimes, it comes back to me. (*sees her expression*) What is it?

Blair. Gus, let's make a pact.

Gus. We already have.

Blair. Let's not ever talk about this again. (*He doesn't answer. She traces some lines on his face with her fingers.*) You look tired, baby. (*He nods.*) I poured you some wine. (*She moves to table.*) I only poured one because my hand was trembling too much. (*She picks up bottle, looks at label.*) You do drink red, don't you? This is something I've been saving for a very special occasion.

Gus. I prefer white, Blair. (*a split second's hesitation*)

Blair. Oh, all right — white it is. But I think you should know you've just turned down some of my very best private stock. (*She starts towards kitchen.*) I have some white on ice in the kitchen.

Gus. Blair? (*She turns.*) I'll drink the red.

Blair. It's no trouble to get the —

Gus. No, the red is fine. (*She moves to table, pours a glass for herself, sits. She indicates for him to sit opposite her. He takes off holster and gun, puts it over chair, sits. She raises glass.*)

Blair. Gus — a toast. "Si on commence a prende Vienne — prendez Vienne."

Gus. What does that mean?

Blair. Drink up and I'll tell you. (*They drink.*) Is this as good as I think it is?

(*MAGGIE silently appears from behind the curtain some three feet to the rear of GUS. She is holding a poker in her hand.*)

Gus. What does the toast mean, Blair?

BLAIR. Well, it's not really a toast. It's something Napoleon said. Rough translation, "If you start to take Vienna—take Vienna." (*These are the last words he hears as MAGGIE clubs him from behind. He slumps down onto the table. BLAIR examines him.*)

MAGGIE. (*shakily*) Is he out?

BLAIR. Yes, but I don't know for how long. (*BLAIR and MAGGIE drag him to the jacuzzi, put him on the floor and then roll him into the open jacuzzi. His body disappears with a splash. BLAIR crosses to the jacuzzi controls, presses button and the jacuzzi top closes over him. She then turns the tap on.*)

MAGGIE. How long will it take?

BLAIR. (*checks watch*) Not long. I've already timed it. It fills very quickly. (*BLAIR moves to turn out the rest of the lights so that the set is now only lit by moonlight, the occasional flash of lightning and the firelight.*)

MAGGIE. Why are you turning the light out?

BLAIR. If anybody drives by I don't want them to see in. (*The two sit cross-legged on the floor by the closed jacuzzi top. BLAIR stares at the jacuzzi pensively as MAGGIE regards her with a curious expression.*)

MAGGIE. (*finally*) You do believe in the telling detail, don't you? (*BLAIR looks up from jacuzzi.*) What was all that about my car not starting?

BLAIR. The probable specific that makes a lie believable. It's all in the mixture.

MAGGIE. I think you missed your calling. You should write.

BLAIR. I do. I just don't put my fantasies on paper. But, even in a fantasy it's the details that give it texture.

MAGGIE. I didn't know you knew so much about cars.

BLAIR. I do.

MAGGIE. Did you tamper with the brakes or the steering on your first husband's car? Is that why he went over the cliff?

BLAIR. (*finally*) It was an accident, Maggie.

MAGGIE. Will I ever know what *you're* thinking, Blair?

BLAIR. No. Part of my appeal. (*a small pause*)

MAGGIE. Why did you hug him? (*BLAIR looks at her.*) You hugged him so *hard*. Why did you do that?

BLAIR. I was sorry to see him go.

MAGGIE. What?

BLAIR. I liked him, Maggie; he was very special. That much was true. That's why he believed me.

MAGGIE. I thought you used him because he was middle-aged and vulnerable.

BLAIR. No.

MAGGIE. What was so special about him?

BLAIR. (*finally*) He was smart, funny, decent—but with just enough larceny to make him human—and I liked him very much. (*She raises her glass at jacuzzi.*) Goodbye, Gus. (*MAGGIE watches with incredulous eyes as tears roll down BLAIR's cheeks.*)

MAGGIE. Jesus, I don't believe it. You're crying.

BLAIR. I told you—I liked him.

MAGGIE. Enough to *cry* over him?

BLAIR. Sometimes I get carried away.

MAGGIE. You just *killed* him!

BLAIR. He gave me no choice.

MAGGIE. What are you talking about?

BLAIR. (*finally*) Maggie; allow me my secrets. (*She breaks the eye contact but MAGGIE doesn't take her eyes from her.*)

MAGGIE. You believe that you can manipulate the whole world, don't you? That you're smarter than everybody.

BLAIR. (*evenly*) No, I don't think that because that would be stupid. I never underestimate anybody.

MAGGIE. Don't ever underestimate me, Blair.

BLAIR. I promise.

MAGGIE. Do you love me?

BLAIR. Of course. (*There is a clap of thunder and some lightning outside. MAGGIE shudders.*)

MAGGIE. Could we get this over with? I'm beginning to feel like one of the witches in the Scottish play. (*BLAIR checks watch, nods, stands, and moves to jacuzzi controls. MAGGIE also stands. BLAIR hyperventilates slightly.*)

BLAIR. All right, now for the — hard part. (*She presses button and crosses to beside MAGGIE as the top slowly slides open. The two women stare down into the widening jacuzzi; the light from inside reflecting up on their faces creating a strange eerie effect. It is now fully open and the two women peer down. A pause. Quietly:*) Oh, my God.

(*The two women are transfixed as GUS, everything except his hair and face soaking wet, rises slowly out of the jacuzzi. He regards the speechless BLAIR for a moment.*)

GUS. Blair, I think I can definitely say you are under arrest. (*He moves away, patting his pockets.*) Now if the damned card isn't too soggy I'll read you your rights.

MAGGIE. I need a drink. (*She crosses to get drink but BLAIR remains motionless.*)

GUS. Is there a towel around here? I tell you I'm too old a geezer for these kind of shenanigans. (*BLAIR moves over to chair as if to get towel.*) You got a towel?

BLAIR. Here, Gus. (*He turns to find BLAIR with his gun in her hand. It is pointed right at him.*)

GUS. (*finally*) Don't do it, kid. Put the gun down, Blair. (*He slowly starts to move towards her.*) It's not worth the price. How are you going to get away with this?

BLAIR. I'll think of something.

GUS. No, I don't believe you're going to do it, Blair. (*BLAIR fires at GUS. There is a loud gunshot explosion and GUS stops in his tracks but then keeps moving, takes the gun from BLAIR.*) Blanks. Last time I used it was when I was a starter at the Kiwanis track meet. (*a pause*)

BLAIR. I know. I heard you tell Doris. You can hear everything from upstairs.

GUS. If you knew why did you fire it?

BLAIR. Sometimes I get carried away.

(*He watches her as she moves over to couch, not sure if she is telling the truth or not. DORIS, gun in hand, and carrying a large towel and old sweat suit, enters.*)

GUS. There you are. What kept you?

DORIS. Who fired the gun? Are you okay?

GUS. Just a little damp around the edges. (*To BLAIR*) Oh, in case you're wondering, Doris turned the water off at the main.

DORIS. Here, put this on before you catch cold. (*She helps him off with wet clothes during following.*)

GUS. Thanks, kid. (*BLAIR turns to look at him.*)

BLAIR. Why, Gus?

GUS. I didn't have a case.

BLAIR. You still don't. You don't have any witnesses.

GUS. Oh, yes I do now. I have Maggie.

BLAIR. You really think Maggie would testify against me?

GUS. I do now that she knows you tried to kill her.

BLAIR. Why would she think that?

GUS. Because the only reason you had me knocked out with a poker is because you knew the pills I gave you were harmless. And the only way you would have known they were harmless is if you had tried them on Maggie and they hadn't worked. (*BLAIR turns to MAGGIE.*)

BLAIR. Maggie, it's not true! (*MAGGIE looks at her for a moment.*)

MAGGIE. Sometimes you underestimate people, Blair. (*as BLAIR goes to speak*)

GUS. Too late, kid. Last night I told her how you planned to kill her. She didn't believe me. Not until tonight when she realized you'd put the pills in her wine.

BLAIR. How?

GUS. She could taste them. They were salt pills. (*He shrugs.*) All I wanted was a witness. But then when you found out the pills didn't work you realized that I'd double-crossed you so you modified the plan slightly. (*unbelievingly*) You were really willing to go either way, weren't you?

BLAIR. I thought we wanted the same things, Gus.

GUS. (*steadily*) I found another way to take Vienna, kid. Anyway, when Maggie phoned me and told me what you planned to do I decided to go for the extra point. (*He gingerly feels his head; to MAGGIE:*) Did you have to hit me that hard?

MAGGIE. I'm an actress, not a stuntwoman. (*GUS looks at BLAIR.*)

GUS. I'll tell you the truth, kid—I'm a little disappointed in you. You really got sloppy. After you found out I'd fed you useless pills didn't it occur to you that I might have confided in my colleagues?

BLAIR. No.

GUS. Why not?

BLAIR. I thought you loved me.

GUS. Lady, you're a real daisy. (*a small pause*)

DORIS. I think we can all go in the same car.

MAGGIE. (*drily*) Why not? I mean we're all friends. And we have so much to talk about. (*She moves to door, turns.*) Hey, I have this great idea. Why don't we all meet a year from now? (*DORIS and MAGGIE exit but BLAIR turns back.*)

BLAIR. (*with genuine curiosity*) Gus, why didn't you go along with me?

GUS. I wanted to be rich and famous again. (*He gives a little regretful "sorry about that" shrug.*) This case is going to make a hell of a book.

BLAIR. I have two children. They have no father.

GUS. You going to throw yourself on the mercy of the court? I do believe that's a definition of hutzpah.

BLAIR. I'll be out in three years. I might even get a suspended sentence.

GUS. I'll still be rich and famous. (*She watches him as he heads for his coat.*)

BLAIR. Gus, you want to be really rich? Really famous? (*He turns to look at her.*) You write a book, maybe it will sell, maybe it won't. But do you want a *guaranteed* best seller? (*Despite himself he has become curious.*) Collaborate with me.

GUS. (*thrown*) What?

BLAIR. A collaboration between the detective and the murderer. We'll write alternate chapters. The murderer's point of view, the detective's point of view! It's *never* been done before, Gus. (*He is staring at her with unbelieving eyes.*) I even have the title — "Fatal Attraction" — and the book cover — a woman's stiletto high heel treading on a red heart with one or two drops of blood dripping from the heart. Who could resist it?

GUS. (*faintly*) Who indeed?

BLAIR. Do you have any idea what a book like that would be worth? Ten million dollars — conservative estimate. Book of the Month — paperback rights — we could presell the movie rights tomorrow. (*He is looking at her with a mixture of amazement and admiration.*)

GUS. You just don't quit, do you? You just keep coming.

BLAIR. It would keep us together, Gus. Isn't that what you really want? (*He doesn't answer. She moves to him.*) Here's something to help you make up your mind. (*She embraces him, kisses him. Behind his back we see she is holding a knife she has picked up from the table. It is pointed at GUS' back. They break but stay in embrace.*) Help at all?

GUS. I — I wouldn't bet too big on this one, kid. (*The knife wavers slightly. Is she going to use it?*)

BLAIR. (*finally*) Big? I'm betting my life on it. (*She breaks embrace, hands him knife.*) Here. Don't ever let anyone tell you I have a cold heart. (*She leaves a bemused GUS, moves to door, turns. Quietly persuasive:*) Pick up the phone, Gus. Phone your publisher — ask him if I'm right. Don't take my word for it. Check with him. (*a beat*) Think about it, Gus. Think about it. (*She flashes her beaming, vulnerable smile at him and exits. He looks after her and then at phone, his expression thoughtful. He moves to it, absently fingers dial. DORIS enters.*)

DORIS. Gus, what the hell are you doing?

GUS. I'll be right there. (*She waits.*) I'm just thinking about something. (*She exits. He is staring at phone. He starts out but stops, turns back, and is staring at phone as the curtain falls and the play is over.*)

THE END

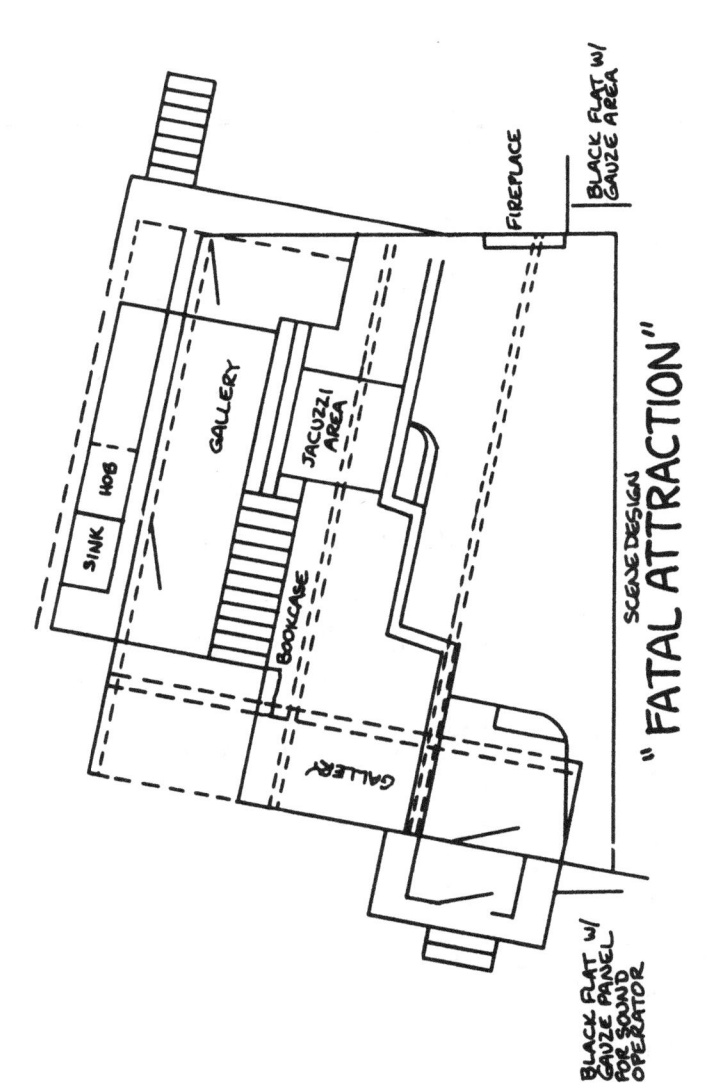

SINK | HOB

GALLERY

JACUZZI AREA

BOOKCASE

GALLERY

FIREPLACE

BLACK FLAT W/ GAUZE AREA

BLACK FLAT W/ GAUZE PANEL FOR SOUND OPERATOR

SCENE DESIGN

"FATAL ATTRACTION"

93

Also By

Bernard Slade

AN ACT OF THE IMAGINATION

FLING!

I REMEMBER YOU

RETURN ENGAGEMENTS

ROMANTIC COMEDY

SAME TIME, NEXT YEAR

SPECIAL OCCASIONS

YOU SAY TOMATOES